"Do you love him?"

Had anyone told Maddie a few weeks ago that Sean Arteaga would ask that question of her, she would have scoffed. "I loved the man I got engaged to. But did he exist?"

"Maybe he changed. People do."

She brought her gaze up to his. "And isn't that scary? How do you know who will change and who won't?"

"Have your other friendships changed?"

Maddie adjusted herself on the sofa, staring at the dark window. "My best friends, no. And Kayla, my business partner, she's been a rock."

Kayla had been great. Swooping in to protect her, arranging matters so that she didn't have to deal with brides until she felt stronger.

Silence fell, and Maddie appreciated the fact that despite everything, they could enjoy a quiet moment. She let out a soft breath, then she and Sean turned their heads at the exact same moment, their gazes connecting.

There was no mistaking what he was thinking.

Dear Reader,

A Sweet Montana Christmas includes so many of my favorite tropes—opposites attract, grumpy hero with a heart of gold, Montana ranch!—that the story almost wrote itself. I love it when that happens.

Maddie Kincaid is a recently jilted bride who plans to spend Christmas caretaking a guest ranch. Sean Arteaga has just seen the end of his rodeo career, and has the scars to prove it. He, too, is spending the holidays caretaking the guest ranch. The only problem is that they don't know that the other will be on the ranch, and they have a bit of a history. They didn't see eye to eye ten years ago when they'd worked on the guest ranch and there doesn't seem to be much hope of that happening now...until they start prepping the ranch for Christmas and holiday magic takes over—or tries to. Sean and Maddie fight the magic, but it is Christmas and eventually...well, you know. Things just have a way of working out sometimes.

I hope you enjoy *A Sweet Montana Christmas*, the second book in The Cowgirls of Larkspur Valley series. If you haven't, please consider following me on Facebook at facebook.com/jeannie.watt.1.

Happy reading!

Jeannie Watt

HEARTWARMING

A Sweet Montana Christmas

—

Jeannie Watt

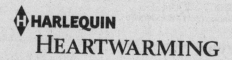

HARLEQUIN

HEARTWARMING

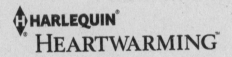

ISBN-13: 978-1-335-47547-3

A Sweet Montana Christmas

For questions and comments about the quality of this book,
please contact us at CustomerService@Harlequin.com.

Harlequin Enterprises ULC
22 Adelaide St. West, 41st Floor
Toronto, Ontario M5H 4E3, Canada
www.Harlequin.com

Printed in U.S.A.

Jeannie Watt lives on a smallish hay and cattle ranch in southwest Montana with her husband and parents. When she's not writing, Jeannie keeps herself busy sewing, baking and feeding lots of animals. She grew up in north Idaho, graduated from the University of Idaho with degrees in geology and education and then spent the next thirty years living in rural northern Nevada. Twenty-two of those years were spent off the grid, which gave her a true appreciation for electricity when she moved to the family ranch in Montana after retiring from teaching. If you'd like to contact Jeannie, please visit her Facebook page at facebook.com/jeannie.watt.1.

Books by Jeannie Watt

Harlequin Heartwarming

The Cowgirls of Larkspur Valley

Home with the Rodeo Dad

Sweet Home, Montana

Montana Homecoming
Montana Dad
A Ranch Between Them

Her Montana Cowboy

Harlequin Western Romance

Montana Bull Riders

The Bull Rider Meets His Match
The Bull Rider's Homecoming
A Bull Rider to Depend On
The Bull Rider's Plan

Visit the Author Profile page
at Harlequin.com for more titles.

I would like to dedicate this book
to my dad, Jack Swanson.
I miss you, Dad.

CHAPTER ONE

"MADDIE...ARE YOU OKAY?"

Maddie Kincaid, who'd been staring at the Christmas wreath above the café counter without really seeing it, gave a small start. "I'm fine."

She flashed a smile at Holly Freely, the petite red-headed owner of the café located two doors down from Spurs and Veils, the Western bridal boutique Maddie owned with her partner, Kayla Metcalf. Despite her best efforts, she felt her bright smile start to droop at the corners. She'd have to work on that.

Holly frowned as she pulled out a chair and lowered herself into it, glancing around the café to make certain no one needed her attention before saying, "You don't look fine. I..."

Her voice trailed as Maddie lifted her right hand from where it had been covering her left, which now felt strange without her engagement ring. Life felt strange without her engagement ring.

"Your ring," Holly said before raising her gaze. "Are you having it cleaned?"

Maddie could tell that motherly Holly knew the answer, but still hoped that Maddie would say yes, the ring was at the jewelers.

Holly was a sweetheart, which was a problem because Maddie was not in the mood for sympathy. She should have headed straight home to continue packing after leaving work, but dealing with happy bridal clients had made for a bad day—a constant reminder of the stab in the heart she'd received less than a week ago. She'd needed to decompress and put something in her empty stomach, so she'd headed to the café.

Holly put a hand on Maddie's, silently encouraging her to spill.

"Cody—" Her voice threatened to crack, and since Maddie Kincaid did not cry in public, she paused to take a breath, gain control.

"You broke up?"

Maddie nodded, still not trusting her voice. Finally she said, "Six weeks before our wedding."

"Oh, sweetie. I'm so sorry." Holly glanced over her shoulder as a group of teens came in wearing red velvet Santa hats and headed to a table at the rear of the café. "Your deposits?"

"Not looking good," she said. "But hey… I guess it's worth several thousand dollars to not marry the wrong guy, right?"

The wrong guy who up until a week ago had appeared to be the right guy. The perfect guy.

Come to find out, the way he'd been distancing himself hadn't been a matter of prewedding jitters. He'd been having serious second thoughts. Thoughts he'd finally shared.

He'd broken the news during a drive after an oddly stilted dinner with his aunt and uncle. He'd even said those deadly words, *It's not you. It's me*.

Days later, Maddie still felt numb. Numb, teary, exhausted.

She couldn't afford exhaustion. She still had to move her belongings off Cody's family ranch, where she'd been renting a refurbished 1950s trailer house that made her smile every time she walked in the door. Ironically, Cody didn't live on the ranch, but Maddie did. Even though Cody's aunt had told her that she could stay as long as she wanted after hearing the sad news, Maddie couldn't. It wasn't fair to her or to Cody's aunt and uncle, and it wasn't fair for her to have to live with constant reminders of what she no longer had.

She was not going to be Mrs. Cody Marsing. Not going to be a wife and partner.

"You're the first person I've told who isn't a family member or business partner," she said. She'd called Whit and Kat, her best friends, the morning after the breakup, but since neither had spent Thanksgiving in Larkspur this year, they were not able to offer in-person moral support.

"I'll keep it quiet."

"Don't. I want people to know." Making the calls to her invitees over the past two days had been difficult enough without having to explain to casual acquaintances that the golden couple were no longer gold.

The teens began rattling their menus and Holly rolled her eyes. "If they weren't regulars and so darned cute, I'd have a word." She got to her feet. "Do you want your usual?" A BLT on wheat, light mayo.

"I'm not that hungry. Just tea and a pastry."

"I'll get you something with a lot of icing."

Maddie's stomach, which usually did a happy dance at the mention of sugar, roiled.

"Could you make it to go?" she asked. "I have a lot of packing to do." And it might be a bit until she could choke down an entire iced pastry. Apparently being jilted was an effective diet aid.

Holly's eyes went wide at the mention of packing. "Oh…" she said as she put two and two together and realized that Maddie would be moving off the Marsing Ranch. "Do you have a place to stay?"

If she said no, then Holly would start searching out living spaces, and right now all Maddie wanted to do was to be alone. Very, very alone. Which was why she hadn't immediately taken up her friend Kat Farley's offer to move in with her until she found a new place. If things got serious, as in if she couldn't find a place, then she'd take Kat's offer. Until then, she'd fall into her old habit of assuming everything would work out in the end—despite the recent proof that it did not.

"I'm good."

Holly gave her a mom look, then turned toward the table of teens who started chanting, "Holly... Holly..." while lightly banging the silverware.

"Excuse me. I have to do bodily harm to some patrons," Holly said with a wink.

After Holly left, Maddie pulled out her phone and pretended to read. Coming here was a mistake. Going to work had been a mistake. Upon hearing the news, Kayla had offered to bring in her niece Elsa, to take Maddie's place for a few weeks. Now that she'd gone through two brutal days of Black Friday sales, dress fittings and happy talk, she was seriously considering it.

Why not?

She'd always been strict with herself. Once a commitment was made, she followed through. If she had a deadline, she met it. No excuses. She was committed to her business, but given the circumstances, and Kayla's cooperation, why not give herself a break?

The only reason she could think of was that she never had. When one grew up with grandparents who expected excellence and a can-do attitude, that's what one ended up with.

But maybe, this once, she could say stuff it, and do something for herself.

Like hide out and mope for a few weeks.

Maddie set the phone on the table. She had savings, and a month off from the job might help her gain perspective, because right now, she didn't feel like being involved in the wedding world. Happy endings weren't guaranteed, and she was in the business of pretending that they were.

What percentage of her clientele had ended up divorced?

Now, that was a statistic she'd like to see.

She folded her hands again, only this time she put her left on top of the right. *Look everyone. No ring.*

Maddie pulled her hands into her lap, out

of sight. She wasn't snarky by nature. That was her friend Whitney Fox's job. Kat Farley, the third member of their triad, was the logical one. Maddie was the optimist. The sunshine girl.

Maddie's mouth tightened. She was done with sunshine for a while.

Holly approached the table with a go cup, a paper bag and a concerned look. "No charge."

Maddie didn't argue. Not charging made Holly feel like she was helping, and Holly needed to help as much as Maddie needed to be alone.

"Thanks, Holl."

"You take care." It was an order.

"I will." She'd take care, and assess and generally put her life back in order. And she was going to try to do it out of the sight of prying eyes, where she didn't have to wear her positive face.

Maddie Kincaid was going to find herself a holiday hideaway where she could lick her wounds, be as snarky as she wanted and not have to face down yet another happy bride who was getting what Maddie thought she'd had.

SEAN ARTEAGA TOLD himself that the pain in his leg was all in his head. Yes, the leg was mangled and yes, the nerves were still healing, but the more he let pain define him, the greater the pain became—something he'd learned during his career as a bronc rider. When a guy started at the age of fifteen, thirty-two was ancient and Sean felt just that. Ancient.

He hadn't felt that way until a gelding by the name of Hopper slammed him into the gates on his last ride two months ago, smashing his leg and opening up the side of his face, but now…now he felt it.

And he wasn't going to let "it" define him.

That said, he wished he knew what was going to define him. That was going to take some thought, and fortunately, thanks to his friend and former employer Max Tidwell, who'd also been one of his sponsors early on, he had a place to do that.

He slowed as he hit the outskirts of Larkspur, Montana. The little town had grown, but thanks to most new Montanans choosing to live in the larger cities, it was still a sleepy place, with Christmas decorations attached to every available surface.

Christmas.

He'd planned on skipping the holidays this year because he was not in the mood, but then the offer came from Max. Would he be interested in keeping an eye on the guest ranch—which was closed for the season— and keeping tabs on Max's sixteen-year-old son, Dillon, who wouldn't be traveling to Mexico for the Christmas holidays due to wrestling practice?

Sean would be delighted.

And he would probably also celebrate Christmas because of Dillon, but in a low-key way. Maybe he'd cook his famous Christmas tacos for the kid.

He stopped at the first of two stoplights and studied the people heading in and out of stores. Thanksgiving had come and gone the week prior, and now Christmas shopping was in full swing. And, for the third year in a row, he had no one to buy a gift for. He'd lost his parents in his early twenties, and after messing up a relationship with a rather awesome woman, he was on his own.

You like it that way.

He did. No commitments meant not disappointing anyone, as he'd disappointed Shay more than once when it came to meshing their lives. There was nothing wrong with Shay wanting him to settle… and there was nothing wrong with him wanting to continue his career until he couldn't. He had sponsors, a decent winning streak and an NFR title. He also had no career to fall back on.

That last little detail had bitten him in the butt.

His most recent career had unexpectedly ended, *thank you, Hopper.* He needed to find a new livelihood—which he was actively working on—because no one wanted a washed-up bronc rider with a limp and scarred face as their spokesperson. The jeans deal and the cowboy coffee deal were now sweet memories.

He reached up to rub the injured side of his face as the light changed. It still itched, but eventually that would pass—

or so he hoped, judging by the thick scar that had formed on his shoulder from his very first rodeo injury. Another wreck that had brought the audience to their feet, but he'd walked away from that one.

From now on, he'd be limping away from anything left in his wake.

Once he hit the city limits, he started scouting the highway for the turnoff to Lucky Creek Guest Ranch, which was only a few miles out of town. It'd been ten years since he'd worked at the place, and even then, the exit had snuck up on him.

There.

He slowed and turned, his lights flashing over the sign. He only hoped that when he left Lucky Creek Guest Ranch, he'd know where he was going and what he was going to do. And until he did, he'd earn his keep by feeding livestock, keeping an eye on the water pipes and riding herd on a teen.

Piece of cake.

CHIN UP, MADDIE. You've got this.

She didn't, and it was stupid to try to trick herself into believing that she did.

She'd been walloped out of the blue and it was going to take time and tears to work through the fallout. She blinked. Hard.

Looking back, the signs had been there. Cody had been distant. Distracted. His smiles hadn't touched his eyes the way they once had. Why hadn't she paid attention to those signs?

Because she'd glossed over things. Came up with excuses. Convinced herself that if she maintained her positive attitude that everything would turn out right in the end.

Maybe it had.

Maddie shushed her inner voice, even as a small part of her acknowledged the truth there. She'd think about it later. Right now she wanted to get her stuff loaded before Cody's aunt and uncle returned to the ranch. They'd already exchanged awkward goodbyes after Maddie turned down the offer to stay there for as long as she needed. She couldn't do that. Not with Cody coming and going to help with the winter feeding and such. He was quite literally the last person she wanted to see.

She swabbed the mop over the floor of

the trailer, determined to leave it ready for the next occupant, and there would be one, since the Marsings depended on rental income to help with ranch expenses. Once the mopping was done and the cleaning equipment stashed in the back seat of her small truck, she double-checked the latch of the rented utility trailer which now held all of her belongings. It was secure. She was not.

She stood for a moment, her hand still on the latch, her chin down, staring at the snowy ground near her feet.

Then she shook her head and dropped her hand. *Turn the page. Turn it now.*

She fished in her pocket for her phone and dialed Max Tidwell. It was a long shot, but she'd worked for Max on his guest ranch during college breaks and because the Lucky Creek Guest Ranch was also a wedding venue, she'd maintained contact over the years.

The guest ranch closed for the winter in October, with the exception of the Chamber of Commerce Open House, and Max and his family always traveled to their home on the Mexican coast for Christmas, so maybe, just maybe, she could stay there. It wasn't like he didn't have a lot of extra beds.

Max answered on the first ring, and it took Maddie a second to find her voice.

"Hi, Max. It's Maddie Kincaid." She sucked in a breath. "I have a big ask."

"Anything you want," he said in a voice that told her he'd heard the news. Of course he had. The local bridal boutique owner being jilted just before the wedding was news, and the citizens of Larkspur, like those of any other smallish community, loved news, aka gossip.

"I need a place to stay for a few weeks."

The silence at the other end of the line made her stomach knot up. She was about to say, *Never mind*, when Max said, "Of course you can stay here for a few weeks. Shirl and I are headed south, but Dillon's staying due to sports."

"Maybe he'd like company?"

Another hesitation. "I have an idea playing in my head," Max said slowly, as if he were still piecing things together. "Where are you staying tonight?"

"I'm staying on the Farley Ranch until I get situated somewhere else." Kat's family had offered her temporary quarters, but the ranch was teeming with activity and people, and it was exactly the opposite of what she needed to get things sorted out in her brain. But a teenager with sports practice—that she could deal with.

She hadn't seen much of Dillon since he'd been an adorable eight-year-old, but she imagined that now he was probably deep into the leave-me-alone teen years. The fact that he wasn't going to spend Christmas with his family in Mexico spoke to that.

"If you have time to stop by this evening, I think we can work something out."

"Thank you, Max." She spoke quietly, but her voice vibrated with gratitude. "As luck would have it, I'm free this evening."

So very free.

"Great. Come on by. Shirl's just finishing up some Christmas cookies while Dill's at wrestling practice. She's hiding them in the freezer so that he doesn't eat them all to-morrow."

Maddie smiled in spite of herself. Teenage boy.

"Thanks, Max. I'll see you soon."

"You can stay the night if you like, rather than head out on winter roads later."

"I would like that. Thanks again."

After contacting the Farleys to tell them that she was staying at the Lucky Creek Guest Ranch and thanking them for the offer of a bed, Maddie set out, hyper-focusing on the road and trying to keep emotions from breaching her defenses as she drove away from the Marsing Ranch for the last time.

You don't have this, but given time, you will. You're tough.

Maddie blinked again; the tears weren't as close to spilling as before. She *was* tough and now that life had given her a good smack, she was going to draw on that toughness and stop pretending things were sunny when they were not. She was going to embrace life, warts and all.

She gripped the steering wheel more firmly as the thought took hold, her mouth tightening into a flat, determined line.

It was time for the sunshine girl to take a hike. There was a new Maddie in town.

"IT'S OKAY TO look at my face, you know." Sean gave Dillon Tidwell, Max's sixteen-year-old son, a smile that hurt his cheek. Even when he tried smiling on one side, he felt the pull of the healing muscles from temple to mid-jawline. The rodeo accident had occurred in mid-October and the stitches were long gone, but he still felt like if he smiled, he would damage something.

That worked because, for the most part, Sean didn't feel like smiling. But he was now. For the kid.

"Sorry." Dillon gave Sean a sheepish grin as he helped unload Sean's meager belongings from the back seat of his extended cab truck. When Sean had last seen the kid, two years ago, he'd been three inches shorter and had sported a head of blond curls. Now the teen's hair was cropped short, and he moved with the casual grace of an athlete. Big change.

"No need to be sorry," Sean said. "Feel free to look. No skin off my nose."

"'Cause it's grown back?" Dillon said.

Sean laughed. "How'd you guess?"

"The picture of you after the wreck was all over. Your face looked like hamburger."

"Felt that way, too." Sean ran a hand over his cheek. The surgeon had done a great job of putting his face back together. He wished they'd had the same luck with his leg, but complications had slowed the healing there, which meant that he'd have a permanent limp. Or so the doctors said. The cast had been off for a little more than a week and the leg was weak as could be, but he was going to work on that. Grit and determination, cleverly disguised behind a devil-may-care attitude, had gotten him this far, and would see him through this challenge, too. Only he was dropping the devil-may-care part.

"So, Dad wants to talk to you after you get settled. He said five o'clock if that works. There's something he wants to run by you."

"Any idea what?"

Dillon shook his head, then dropped the

duffel beside the unmade bed. "Need help with the sheets before I head to practice?"

Sean wasn't one who asked for help, and the offers of assistance put his back up in a serious way since the wreck, as if he was no longer capable of handling the day-to-day. But help from Dillon felt different.

"Sure," he said.

"Stand back." Dillon lifted the bedding from the double bed and set it on the chair before taking a sheet and expertly flipping it so that it spread over the top of the mattress. He walked around the bed, tucking as he went. "We don't use fitted sheets," he said as he jammed the fabric between the mattress and box springs, stretching it tight. "Kind of a pain sometimes, but it works better for inventory. We don't have to have matched sets."

"Ah."

After the bottom sheet was tucked, the kid continued making the bed, his movements quick and efficient.

"You've done this before," Sean stated.

Dillon shot him a quick smile. "A few times."

Sean stood back and let the boy work. "Thanks," he said after Dillon smoothed the top cover with a flourish.

"No problem." He looked around the cabin. "You should be comfortable here."

Spoken like a guest ranch host. Sean felt the pull on his cheek again as he smiled. "Tell your dad I'll be over at five."

"Will do. Just…well…if he tries to talk you into doing the open house, see if you can talk him out of it."

"What open house?"

Dillon rolled his eyes. "Every year we're part of this big deal thing that the Larkspur Chamber of Commerce puts on the first Saturday in December. But this year they changed the date, so we can't do it because the parental units will be in Mexico. It's expensive to change vacation plans, you know."

"I don't think your dad is going to ask me to host an open house."

Dillon unabashedly ran his gaze over Sean, taking in his scarred face and his lopsided stance as he rested his bad leg instead of sitting.

"You might be right." He nodded. "I hope you're right. You cannot believe what a pain it is getting the main lodge ready for this thing. But it's good PR, so every year..." Dillon rolled his eyes again. "I thought I'd dodged this bullet when they changed the date."

"I'm pretty sure you're safe," Sean said. He hoped so anyway, because if Max asked him to ramrod an open house, he would. He owed the man for giving him a place to stay while he figured out his next moves in life.

"Guess we'll find out. See you at five."

"See you then." Sean waited until the door closed behind the teen before squeezing his forehead with one hand.

Please, Max. No open house.

His days of entertaining crowds were over.

CHAPTER TWO

SNOW STARTED TO fall as Maddie drove to the Lucky Creek Guest Ranch, big fat flakes that melted almost before they touched the windshield. Maddie didn't bother with the wipers until she drove under the wood-and-wrought-iron arch that marked the entrance to the guest ranch. By that time the snow started coming down harder and the flakes no longer melted, but instead accumulated. The wipers cut through them, but the head-lights bounced off the wall of white ahead of her, making her glad that she'd decided to come earlier than planned. She'd told Max six o'clock, but she'd been able to wrap things up with Kayla more quickly than she'd thought, which made her frown in retrospect.

When did Kayla *not* consider all possible consequences, pro and con, before acting?

When she had a sad-faced business

partner who wasn't buying into the happy-happy-joy-joy wedding thing. A partner who'd been on the edge of tears a couple of times that day while a young bride-to-be excitedly tried on every dress in the place.

Yeah. She could understand why Kayla had all but pushed her out the door after Maddie confessed that she wanted to take a few weeks off.

Make it six, Kayla had said firmly. *Elsa is available until mid-January, so you may as well take advantage.*

And so she was. If Max, who usually stayed south until mid-February, wanted her to stay on the guest ranch until his return, she would, driving to work from there.

Maddie slowed, squinting through the snow as she approached the guest ranch lodge, where Max and his family lived in the south wing, the north wing serving as VIP guest rooms. In addition to those rooms, there were six guest cottages and an old-fashioned bunkhouse that served as spillover lodging. The unique round barn on the property served as a wedding venue, which was how Maddie had maintained ties with the Tidwell family. She was not a wedding coordinator per se, but she'd gone the extra mile for clients, sometimes providing last-minute fitting and alterations.

By habit Maddie turned toward the vendor parking area behind the barn, then jerked the steering wheel to the left when a figure appeared out of the snow in front of her.

A cry escaped her lips as the utility trailer she towed took offense at the sudden turn and slid sideways in the wet snow, jolting the truck. Heart pounding, she released her death grip on the steering wheel after the truck came to a stop. A second later she was out of the truck, the wet snow pelting her face.

"Didn't you see me?" a male voice demanded before she could ask if he was all right.

The voice was familiar, yet not. Definitely not one of the Tidwells, but Maddie couldn't see the man's face with the light coming from behind him, turning him into a dark silhouette.

"Obviously not since I don't try to hit people with my truck on purpose. Didn't you see me coming?"

"I did, but my escape options were limited." Maddie frowned, and realized he *could* see her face, because the man's tone shifted as he said, "Maddie Kincaid."

It was a statement. One that tightened her gut as she realized why she knew the voice. She knew it because they'd worked together on this very ranch.

"You," she said simply. Sean Arteaga. The man who'd shaken her world ten years ago, and not in a good way.

"Me," he replied. He was standing oddly, and she noticed that he had a cane in one hand. He followed her gaze. "It helps me get around."

She didn't know how to take the simple statement, so she reiterated, hoping for more of an explanation. "You need help getting around?"

"Yes."

Maddie wiped the snow off her face, then wiped the moisture on her jeans, which were also getting damp. She only had forty zillion questions, the main one being, *Why are you here?*

She asked it out loud.

"I'm here to help out Max while he's in Mexico."

"So am I." A thought hit her. "Are you going to Mexico with him?"

"I'm staying here."

Numbness was becoming a familiar feeling. This was nothing like the cold shock of learning that Cody was calling it quits, but it wasn't a pleasant sensation either. Maddie moistened her lips. "As am I."

"No sh...no kidding."

"I wouldn't kid about that in a snowstorm after almost doing you in." She looked him up and down, then said, "I thought I'd be alone here."

It sounded like an accusation. Maybe it was. Why was he here horning in on her alone time?

"Join the club," he muttered, sounding no happier about the circumstances than she was.

"Hey!"

They turned together toward the lodge

where Dillon Tidwell stood hugging himself. The teen was barely visible through the falling snow.

"Dad wants to know if you're going to stand in the snow or come in where it's warm?"

"We're coming," Sean answered for both of them. Kind of a habit of his from the past.

Maddie forced herself to lower her hackles and a second later, she also forced herself to slow her steps when it became apparent that Sean was dealing with a serious limp. No wonder he wasn't able to get out of the way of the truck.

"Don't wait for me," he all but growled.

Maddie glanced at him, and somehow managed to keep her mouth from falling open as the pole lamp he walked under illuminated the angry Y-shaped scar on the side of his face.

"You're not pretty anymore." The words were blurted out before she could stop them. Sean Arteaga had been a gorgeous guy, confident, charming, overbearing, a touch judgy—at least where Maddie had been concerned.

Her heart rate ramped up as Sean came to a stop and slowly looked her way, a frown bringing his dark eyebrows together. "You've changed, too."

"Life," she said, wishing she'd kept her mouth shut.

He nodded, and without another word began limping toward the lodge. Maddie watched for a moment, wondering if it had been a car wreck or rodeo wreck that had put him in this condition.

Actually, it didn't matter. What did matter was that it appeared that they were both staying at the Lucky Creek Guest Ranch, which meant that Maddie was going to have to find a new hideaway. She was not sharing the holidays with Sean Arteaga.

SEAN HAD TOLD Dillon Tidwell earlier that afternoon that it was fine to stare at him. He wasn't extending the same courtesy to Maddie Kincaid. He did not want her staring at him, but he caught her glancing his way as they took seats in the main hall of the lodge. The lighting was well planned in the big room, so everyone could see his scarred face. No shadows for protection.

You're not pretty anymore.

He'd never been pretty, but he knew that he had physical attributes that women found attractive. He probably still did, with the right woman. Which was not Maddie Kincaid, even though he found his gaze drawn to her when she wasn't looking at him. He'd always thought of her as cute, but some of the softness had left her face, emphasizing her cheekbones and jawline, easing her away from cute and closer to striking.

Actually closer to beautiful, but Sean wasn't going there. Her brown hair was shorter, swinging below her shoulders, and her eyes were that striking color somewhere between green and hazel that had drawn his attention even when he hadn't wanted to notice.

He'd never been one for false optimism, or the sprinkling of sunshine. He could, on a good day, bring himself to believe in silver linings, but he did not delude himself into thinking that everything was rosy—or would shortly be that way—when it obviously was not.

"Sean?"

Max brought him out of his reverie, and he realized that he'd been staring at Maddie, who was now staring back.

"Sorry," he said to no one in particular. "Thousand miles away."

"I'm heading out," Dillon called from the door. "Wish I could stay and make plans, but coach said this meeting is mandatory." He caught Sean's eye and made a slicing motion across his throat, clearly indicating that Sean needed to squelch the open house if it came up. Maddie obviously noticed, but he gave her points for pretending not to.

Shirl handed him a beer and he smiled as he took it. A few seconds later, his gaze strayed back to Maddie. She had changed in the decade since they'd worked together, and not just in a physical way.

Theirs had been an uneasy partnership. He was good with the ranch guests, having developed a persona during his rodeo days, but preferred dealing with horses. Fewer demands. Maddie had been the riding coordinator, responsible for choosing the right mount for each guest, which was what had brought them together for an hour or two every day that there was a trail ride.

She'd been cute and enthusiastic, full of positive energy that he hadn't been able to connect with. He'd been going through a rough spell after a series of losses and hadn't been in the mood to be sprinkled with sunshine. But he'd still been grudgingly drawn to her. Maybe that was why he'd taken her off at the knees during their last real conversation. His fault, not hers.

But something had changed with Maddie. This was not a happy woman sitting a few feet away from him. Even though she smiled as Shirl made small talk, it wasn't the megawatt beam he associated with her.

When Max settled in his ginormous leather chair, he lifted his glass. "Sean. Maddie. Welcome back to Lucky Creek."

"Thank you," Maddie murmured. "I didn't realize when I called that you already had someone here." She shifted her gaze to Sean and he noted that it was a lot more direct than it had been back in the day.

Before Sean could answer, Max gestured at Shirl, who in turn smiled at Maddie. "We invited Sean to stay with Dillon after..."

"My arena wreck," he finished for her.

"Yes. That unfortunate incident."

"I don't want to get in anyone's way," Maddie said, setting her glass down.

"Oh, no no," Shirl said in a rush. "We're thrilled to have both of you here. Sometimes Dill needs double teaming, and Sean doesn't know how long he'll be here, so..." she gave a small shrug as she smiled "... this works out really well. Max and I won't have to hurry home."

"We can still catch the end of the wrestling season in February," Max said.

"But there's one thing," Shirl added, "and before I throw this out there, please understand that 'no' is a perfectly acceptable answer."

"All right," Maddie said, an amused yet cautious note to her voice. Shirl did not, Sean noted, look at him.

"Would you consider hosting the annual Chamber of Commerce open house event here on the ranch? The third weekend in December."

Maddie's mouth opened, then closed again. "I...what's involved?"

Yes. What was involved?

"They usually have the open house the first Saturday in December, and we leave for Mexico a few days later after the cleaning crew and I tidy up. This year, the chamber changed the date to the third week in December, and because of our travel plans, I had to bow out for the first time since the event began fifteen years ago."

"She loves the open house," Max said.

"It's great PR and a lovely way to give back to the community."

Sean watched Maddie's expression as she absorbed this new wrinkle in her be-alone plan. First his unexpected presence and now an open house.

"I'm sorry to put you on the spot," Shirl said apologetically after a few seconds of silence passed. "I thought it was worth the ask, but upon reflection—"

"I'll do it," Maddie said, even though

Shirl had not yet explained what was involved.

"You will?" Shirl beamed at her as her shoulders dropped in a gesture of relief.

"Wait," Max said in a cautionary voice. "She needs to know what she's getting into."

She, not they. Sean found that interesting.

"You're right," Shirl set down her drink and leaned forward with her palms pressed together between her knees. "It's work, but it's really kind of fun. All you have to do is decorate the house, which Dillon knows how to do." She cleared her throat, looking a touch self-conscious as she said, "And… when I heard you were coming, I called the café just in case things worked out, and Holly, bless her heart, will cater for us if I give her the okay tomorrow. So that leaves the hosting duties. I know you're good at that, and frankly, other than greeting the visitors, there's not much involved in the actual event. Just a lot of people coming and going and entering the big raffle."

Shirl, like her husband, did not include

him in the conversation. Was it his scarred face? Or did she simply realize that while he had a ton of experience with the public, he just wanted to hide out for a while?

He went with the latter.

"Of course I'll host," Maddie said, finally smiling her bright smile, but it still wasn't up to megawatt standards. Sean suspected that she was agreeing to the open house only because she was a nice person who hated to rock the boat. She confirmed his suspicion by saying, "I'm happy that I can do something for you guys while you're gone."

"You'll still have weeks of peace and quiet, not counting any trouble Dillon stirs up."

Shirl shifted her attention to Sean. "I'll help," he said before she could excuse him from the event, which he sensed she was about to do. He didn't want to volunteer, but that was the least he could do after failing Dillon by not squashing the open house—as if that was even a possibility. Obviously, it was important to Shirl, and thanks to Maddie it was going to happen. Therefore, he needed to do his part.

"Thank you," Shirl said on a note of surprise, her gaze lingering on his face for a moment longer than necessary.

"Unless you think I'll scare the guests, of course." He spoke lightly, but he was serious. Despite joking about his injuries when they came up in conversation, he felt stupidly self-conscious when every eye turned his way when he walked into a room. Being the center of attention had been normal when he'd been the confident rodeo star being interviewed after a ride or hawking Western wear, coffee and whiskey. Now he was more of a Quasimodo, only without the scoliosis.

Shirl gave him a look. "I know you, remember? You do well in the limelight, but you're not a fan. So no, it has nothing to do with your face."

Sean's eyebrows rose. She did know him. He'd enjoyed his celebrity in small doses, but most of the time he faked it.

"Maybe we should have spoken to you

guys separately," Max said with a slight frown.

"Why?" Sean asked as he and Maddie made a show of whatever-for?, exchanging quick glances, as if to assure their hosts that they had no problem with the way things had been laid out to them.

"We didn't expect both of you to be in residence, obviously," Shirl said. "But when Maddie called, things just fell into place."

So they wouldn't have asked him to host if he'd been there alone. But, yay. Maddie to the rescue.

"Glad to help," Sean said.

Maddie gave him a look which clearly said that she knew he was faking, probably because he'd avoided the guests as much as possible when they'd worked together before, but if Shirl and Max suspected, they didn't let on.

After the matter was settled, they finished their drinks and made small talk, then Sean and Maddie headed out into the storm, he on his way back to the same cabin he'd lived in during his stint at the ranch years ago, and Maddie to get her bags.

"What are you going to do about the U-Haul?" Sean asked when they reached her truck. He'd been wishing that they hadn't left together, because Maddie was obviously slowing her steps so he could keep up, then decided he'd better get used to it. Especially if they were going to collaborate on this open house thing.

"I'm taking it to the Farley Ranch tomorrow and storing my belongings in the old silo before turning it in to the rental place." She smiled a little. "The silo being one of the only buildings on the property that won't catch fire."

"But it might explode," Sean said with a smile. The Farley brothers, whom he knew from local rodeos, were grown, but their reputation for accidental mayhem lived on.

"Let's hope not." She reached for the door handle.

"Need help carrying anything?"

The offer was genuine, but he assumed she'd say no. Instead she said, "Is the cane temporary or permanent?"

"Time will tell."

She pushed the hair back from her forehead, leaving a glistening streak of moisture. "I can handle my own bags."

They faced off for a moment, the flakes coming down hard and fast, covering the shoulders of Maddie's wool jacket. Sean debated, then asked the question that had been niggling at him. A justified question in his book, since they'd be sharing a space.

"Why are you here, Maddie? Did you get evicted?"

"That's *exactly* what happened."

He frowned at her ironic tone, then let it go. "Maybe tomorrow, after the Tidwells leave, we can work out some ground rules."

"Such as?"

"Mutual respect of privacy when we're not working together."

"Are you going to seek me out during off hours?"

"Probably not."

She gave him a grim smile. "Then I do not see how privacy is going to be any kind of an issue between us."

And with that she pulled a single gym bag out of the truck and closed the door. A quick nod in his general direction and then she headed toward the lodge, following the tracks that were rapidly filling with snow.

All right. Not what he'd expected, but what he deserved.

Sean brushed the snowflakes off the front of his coat, then headed toward the cabin. Truth be told, he was having a bit of trouble reconciling this Maddie Kincaid with the younger version who'd tried to cajole him into accepting that it was darkest before the dawn and all that stuff.

She'd been correct. The rodeo career he'd thought was lost after a two-year hiatus following the death of his parents had taken off in a way that even he hadn't foreseen, but that didn't mean that everything always worked out in the end. It hadn't with his love life. He'd been fresh off a broken engagement the first time they'd worked together, and while he could see now that it had been for the best, he'd made the exact same mistake with Shay, causing her to finally give up on him.

Not to dive into self-pity or anything, because he understood that he now had a new normal, but he was having a hard time seeing how his present life was ever going to be as satisfying as his life before the wreck.

He planned to pursue the profession he'd been headed for ten years ago, before his rodeo career took off again, and train to be a diesel mechanic. What he hadn't expected was the popularity of the programs. Despite a healthy price tag, the program he was interested in was full up, so unless someone dropped out, he would be waiting until next January to start training for his new life.

Which in turn left him at loose ends for almost thirteen months.

He needed to find a job, and it had to be one that didn't tax his leg and that paid enough to allow him to keep his tuition money safely in the bank.

That and maybe dodge Maddie Kincaid if possible. The sunshine girl was gone, and in her place was a woman who wanted to be alone. The last thing he needed was to be wondering about what had happened in her life when he should be sorting out his future.

CHAPTER THREE

MADDIE'S ROOM WAS both comfortable and familiar, and as she dropped the gym bag on the white comforter, she felt like she'd come home. In a way, she had, having spent eight months in this room, over the course of two seasons, and she loved both the room and the view over the north pastures.

During the summers that she'd worked on the guest ranch while attending college—two, as opposed to Sean's one— she'd stayed in the main lodge to help with the guests in addition to ramrodding all the trail rides and events that involved horses.

There were other summer employees— general ranch hands who took care of the cattle and the fields; a cook and waitstaff— but she and Sean had been forced into a working relationship due to the overlap of their duties. A working relationship that hadn't been all that cohesive, although she thought they'd faked it well. It didn't appear that Max or Shirl had been aware of any friction between them.

Sean had been something back then. Strikingly handsome and seemingly unaware of the fact, even though the female guests ogled him. Maddie had ogled him herself in the beginning—it was kind of impossible not to—but Sean was off-limits, not only because he was a fellow employee, but because he'd put himself off-limits. With her.

Maddie was good at reading people and with Sean she read "Leave me be." After several attempts to charm him into dropping his guard, something she generally excelled at, she'd given up. But as the summer rolled on, and it became difficult to ignore the fact that he was friendly with everyone else, she'd finally asked him what the deal was. Did he have some kind of issue with her?

He hadn't answered immediately, focusing instead on the saddle he'd been cleaning on the front porch of his cabin when she'd sought him out. When he finally looked up, his blue gaze met hers in a way that made Maddie realize that she was about to hear something she wouldn't like.

"We have different worldviews, Maddie." He held her gaze, as if to convince her of how serious he was. He needn't have bothered. She could tell from his flat tone that he was dead serious.

"How so?"

"I'm a realist and you…"

"Aren't?"

His hand stilled on the saddle fender he'd been polishing, then he started working again.

"I've had a rough couple of years."

He did not elaborate on what made those years rough, nor did she ask, because she'd been half-afraid to. It was only later, after the summer had ended, that she'd casually inquired of Max what Sean's difficulties were and discovered that the man had lost his parents less than two years before, and that he'd been engaged to be married, but that hadn't worked out either.

"I'm sorry to hear that," Maddie said after a beat of silence.

"I'm working through things in my way, in my time." He raised his gaze to meet hers, his expression surprisingly intense. "I don't need or appreciate reminders that life gets better."

At that, Maddie went still. "Your problem with me is that I try to focus on the positive?"

He gave her a tired look. "It's that you're so vocal about it. You practically ran a master's class when Bill Connors—" one of the seasonal ranch hands "—got all those college applications rejected."

But this wasn't about Bill Connors. This was about her using similar tactics with Sean at the beginning of the summer when she'd tried to coax him out of his dark moods, using positive platitudes that he had not taken well.

"Some of us don't believe in one door closing and another opening. Or that tomorrow will be a better day." He pushed the saddle aside and got to his feet. "Some of us simply want to muscle our way through a day without feeling like we have to smile to make *you* feel better."

That had been the gut punch. Smiling to make her feel better.

"It's not like that."

"Isn't it?"

Maddie's sense of being wrongly accused had been difficult to contain, but she'd managed to grind out a response without losing her temper. Much. "I don't need anyone's smile to feel *better*."

Sean had simply raised an eyebrow in a rather maddening way.

"Fine," she'd finally said after battling down another surge of temper. "Wallow in misery and make sure that tomorrow is another crappy day. I don't care."

He hadn't said a word when she'd walked away fuming at his misrepresentation of her motives, and during the final three weeks they'd worked together, she managed to keep their face time at a minimum. She'd half expected him to seek her out and tell her that she'd caught him in a bad moment and that he hadn't meant what he'd said.

He didn't, so she concluded that he'd meant what he'd said. That he believed she was focused solely on her own emotional needs when she tried to cheer people up. And that had stung.

From that point on, Maddie had tempered her impulse to convince people that everything would work out in the end; a belief she'd held on to until Cody dumped her. That was when her worldview had shifted closer to that of Sean Arteaga. Things could work out in the end—but there was no guarantee that they would.

"MOM SENT THESE." Dillon grinned at Sean from the cabin doorway where he stood with a bundle of towels and a can of ground coffee.

"Thanks."

Dillon handed the items over to Sean, then let out a heavy sigh. "You failed me man. The open house is a done deal."

"That was not a battle I could win," Sean said matter-of-factly.

"Did you try?"

"Would you have?"

Dillon shook his head. "That's why I sent you."

"We will be putting on an open house,"

Sean said. "You want to come in and close the door?"

"Oh. Yeah. Sure." Dillon pushed off the doorjamb and stepped into the cabin. "I thought maybe you wanted it open, you know, because it was open."

"Just airing out the place for a couple minutes. It's been closed up for a while."

"Two months. And yeah. The cabins do get stuffy. Dad super insulated them the last time we redid them."

"He runs a good outfit."

"If only it wasn't for the open house thing."

"Where's your Christmas spirit?" Sean asked.

"Oh, I love Christmas. But I can love it without tinsel and stuff, you know?"

"I was on my way out to see about feeding. Your dad said you'd line me out."

"That's why I'm here. I'm supposed to ask if you can drive the tractor with your bad leg, only I'm supposed to be tactful. So, can you?"

Sean had a suspicion that time with Max's son was going to be good for him. The kid was upbeat, but also irreverent, accidentally so about half the time, Sean guessed.

"I can handle the tractor." It was going to hurt, but he could manage.

"Good. Also… Maddie is coming with us tomorrow morning when we feed the cattle."

"Cool." The word came out flatly. Too flatly.

"Right." Dillon gave him a knowing look, which in turn made Sean sigh inwardly.

He was going to have to watch himself. In the two years since he'd last seen Dillon, when he'd been invited for Thanksgiving dinner with the Tidwells before heading to the National Finals Rodeo, the kid had gotten more tuned into undercurrents than he'd been before. In fact, it kind of felt like Dillon was looking for undercurrents.

"She's a good worker," Sean said in a more upbeat tone.

"And pretty. I kind of had a six-year-old's crush on her."

"So did some of the other hands." He recalled that well. People were drawn to her. The guests had loved her. And, he had to say that, looking back, she'd honestly believed that the glass was half-full, which had been annoying when one was operating in glass-half-empty mode.

Dillon gave the room one last look, as if checking for oversights, then said, "It's late. I should head back. Have a good night."

"Will do."

Sean stood at the closed door and watched through the small window as Dillon made his way back to the lodge. There was a light on in the far wing of the lodge. Maddie's light.

He stepped away from the window and ran his palm over the scar on his cheek, then let his hand fall back to his side. He needed to get a grip where Maddie was concerned.

When they'd worked together before, he'd been caught up in his problems and hadn't wanted or needed advice. In other words, he might have behaved like a jerk toward her when she'd simply been doing what came naturally to her. Trying to make people feel better.

So, make it up to her? Or let sleeping dogs lie.

Recalling the way they'd parted the previous evening, with her telling him that she wanted nothing to do with him, he was going with the sleeping dogs.

MADDIE GOT OUT of bed, made her way to the bathroom and splashed water on her face. She'd slept well until her phone had buzzed at six thirty. It had to be either Kat or Whit because no one but a good friend would call that early. She reached for the phone, then set it back on the nightstand when she saw the name on the screen.

Cody.

She let it ring as she lay staring up at the ceiling, glad that he had no idea where she was. It was probably a call concerning deposits, but whatever it was, he could handle it. If it was important, he could text. She hadn't blocked him, but she was thinking about it.

What if he wants to get back together?

Sobering thought.

This was the man she'd been ready to

spend the rest of her life with, and now she didn't want to take his calls. She didn't trust him, and she didn't trust herself.

The call ended after three rings, making Maddie wonder if it had been a butt dial. She'd feel better if it was, but had no way of finding out. Just in case it wasn't, she turned her phone off. A half hour later, when she left the lodge to feed the cows and horses under Dillon's tutelage, she left her phone behind.

New page. New beginning.

She tromped through the fresh snow, following Dillon's tracks until they veered off toward Sean's cabin, then changed course to the equipment barn where the tractors were parked. Beyond the barn a herd of Angus, their black bodies stark against the snowy pasture, waited behind a rime-encrusted fence for their morning meal.

Maddie loved feeding. Her dad had been the foreman of a local ranch until he retired and moved to Maine with his new wife two years ago, so most of her at-home years had revolved around daily chores. But those daily chores never involved working with a guy who set her on edge, and Sean Arteaga did just that. He'd done it when they'd handled the trail horses together and he still had the power to shake her equilibrium— or he would, if Maddie let him.

She wouldn't.

"Maddie. Over here."

She turned toward the tractors as Dillon swept both arms through the air in a full body wave, like she might miss seeing him in his fluorescent green snowboarding jacket. Next to him Sean stood wearing a more sedate winter drover coat. He did not wave.

Grump.

Cut the guy some slack. He's been through a lot.

And for some reason, the only time the two of them seemed to meet up was on the Lucky Creek Ranch after the man had the wind knocked out of him. This time, though, it was more than emotional pain. He was suffering other serious damages. The physical damage was obvious, but it was also possible he'd taken an economic hit having lost his profession.

Well, she wasn't going to tell him to look on the bright side.

She waited until she was almost to the men before saying, "Good morning, guys."

Dillon grinned and Sean gave her a cool nod of acknowledgment, but she had a feeling that he found her flat tone reassuring. She wasn't going to sprinkle pixie dust today. As if she ever would again.

"I take it that your parents got away with no problem?" The snow had been a topic of concern the previous evening. "I didn't hear them go." For the first time since the breakup she'd slept soundly.

"They snuck out at the crack of dawn, and only had to come back once for stuff they forgot. I think that might be a personal best." He put a hand on each of their shoulders. "Now it's just us. The three musketeers." He dropped his hands and stepped back. "What do you say we cancel that open house?"

"It won't kill you to put up some tinsel," Sean said.

Maddie almost smiled at Sean's gruff comment, but rather than give him a reason to be even grumpier, she turned to Dillon, "I guess you'd better line us out."

"Okay." He pushed his hands into his jacket pockets. "Um, let's start with the horses. We're feeding off that far stack there." He pointed to the third of three parallel haystacks. "The first two are alfalfa for the cows. That one's grass. We also have a bunch of waterers to check, and Dad asked me to see that the fences aren't sagging from the last two snowstorms. That said... I have school tomorrow, and practice today at—"

"I'll handle it," Sean said.

"Are you in charge?" The words came out before Maddie could stop them. Not that she would have.

"I'm volunteering."

"Ah."

Judging from the way Sean's dark eyebrows came together, the single syllable expressed more than a well-chosen sentence might have.

"Kids, kids," Dillon said in a light voice, but his expression was serious. "We have a lot to do and no time for personalities."

He was obviously quoting a teacher or coach, but he made a good point. After a quick glance at Sean, Maddie said, "Sean can see to the fences, since he volunteered." She managed not to emphasize the word in the snarky way she wanted to. "I'll start tackling the list that your mom left."

Dillon brought his hands together in front of him then bounced a look between Maddie and Sean. "Okay, now that that's settled, let's get started."

MADDIE KINCAID DIDN'T utter one upbeat word while she and Sean fed first horses, then the cattle under Dillon's watchful eye. On one hand, Sean was relieved that she no longer saw herself as a self-appointed life coach, but on the other, he was uncomfortably aware that they still had a touch of unfinished business, as in the apology he owed her for being so blunt with her ten years ago.

If he'd been in a better state of mind back then, he might have apologized. He'd thought about it, but ultimately refrained, fearing that an apology might take the cork back out of the bottle, and they'd still had weeks to work together.

No, he hadn't been at his finest back then, and while Maddie had overstepped his personal boundaries, he hadn't needed to say what he had in the way he had. He'd shocked her, hurt her, and then had done nothing about it.

He couldn't help but wonder if she'd changed because of him? Dropped the cheerful attitude and became the semi-distant woman now walking beside Dillon a few steps ahead of him as they made their way to the tack shed? Or was this her response to just him, the guy who'd hurt her feelings?

He didn't even know why she was on the ranch for the holidays, which was, of course, a matter between her and the Tidwells. He wasn't even curious.

Liar.

True. He'd come up with a few explanations while he wasn't being curious. She could be between jobs, or houses, or moving back to the area from parts unknown. He might ask Dillon about it at some point.

Right now he was focused on finding out where he stood in the way of tack if he was going to check the fences after the snow. The young gelding he'd ridden when he'd worked at the ranch before, a gray quarter horse by the name of Danny, was still on the property, only now he was a seasoned twelve-year-old. Sean was looking forward to riding him. Looking forward to putting his battered body on a good horse and heading to places where he could simply be alone with his thoughts.

"The guy who cleans the gear and puts it away for the season quit early," Dillon said when Sean ran a finger over a remnant mud splatter on a saddle fender. "As soon as wrestling season is over, guess who gets to oil the saddles and polish the silver?" He stuck a thumb to his chest.

"I'll do it," Sean said. It would help him pass time in the evenings.

"Just like you used to do."

Sean frowned at the kid. "How do you know what I used to do?"

"Kids are observant, and in my case, have a great memory, which is why I'm sporting a 3.8 GPA at this very moment." He twisted his mouth sideways. "You used to clean saddles and every Sunday you waxed your truck."

Those days were long gone, but a shiny truck was important to a twenty-two-year-old cowboy, even one whose heart had been broken in more than one way.

"What else do you remember?" Sean asked curiously.

"I remember that you took care of that orphan kitten until Mom found it a home."

He'd almost forgotten about that because it had only been a matter of days that he'd cared for the little guy, feeding him every couple of hours before some nice lady in Larkspur took over the job.

"Orphan kitten dad, eh?" Maddie said, finally turning on the megawatt smile Sean remembered so well. It was good to see her thaw a little.

"I wear the badge proudly," he said.

She turned to Dillon. "How about me? Any memories?"

"You could burp the alphabet all the way to *P*. Once you made it to *T*."

"Really?" Sean said, shooting her a surprised look.

"I drank a lot of soda when I was young," Maddie replied grudgingly. "And I could make it to Z on a good day."

"How is it that you're still single?" he asked.

He expected Maddie to fire back at him, was kind of looking forward to it, because it was a nice change from affirmations, but instead he got an oddly stricken look and awkward beat of silence.

Dillon cleared his throat as the corners of Maddie's mouth lifted, then quivered when she started to speak. She swallowed, tried again with no better luck, then said, "Excuse me."

The words were barely off her lips before she put her head down and headed toward the door. When it closed behind her, Sean looked at Dillon who was staring at him as if he didn't quite believe what had just happened.

"That was cold."

Sean gave the kid a perplexed look, his

confusion growing at Dillon's expression of dawning understanding.

"You don't know."

"Know what?"

"Oh, man." Dillon pressed his lips together. "The reason she is still single is because the guy she was going to marry dumped her. Like days ago, I guess. They were supposed to get married next month."

Sean uttered a low curse, then glanced at the barn door Maddie had just gone out of.

"Agreed," Dillon said in response to the curse before giving the explanation Sean wished he'd had before he'd put his foot in his mouth. "She asked if she could stay here because she was living on his family ranch and didn't want to stay." He made a gesture. "For obvious reasons."

"I don't blame her." The words came out automatically as Sean quickly worked through next moves in his head. Apologize. Plead ignorance. Let things ride. He dropped his gaze to the straw-strewn planks at his feet, blew out a breath.

If Maddie had no home, she might be here for a while. And he was going to be here until Max and Shirl returned in February. They had at least a month together taking care of livestock, putting on an open house, maybe even celebrating Christmas for Dillon's sake.

"You better apologize. Things will be awkward if you don't."

He raised his eyes to meet Dillon's very serious gaze. "Right."

He was of the opinion that things might become more awkward after he apologized for his faux pas, but in this case, he wasn't going to follow his gut. He was going to do exactly as Dillon said and clear the air between him and Maddie Kincaid.

CHAPTER FOUR

SEAN FOLLOWED MADDIE'S footprints across the unplowed driveway, his leg protesting the slog through deep snow. She was quite a ways ahead of him, striding up the walkway of the lodge as he continued through the snow, her chin held high as if she was determined to keep it together. He hurried his steps, but there was no way he was going to catch up to her.

He had no idea how to tackle this apology, because one of the benefits of not talking much was that he didn't say things he had to apologize for later—Maddie being the exception to the rule.

Maddie was almost to the carved double doors that led directly into the main lodge hall when he called her name. Even at a distance, he saw her back stiffen. Maybe this apology idea was a mistake. Maybe she needed some alone time to compose herself. If so, all she had to do was continue on through the doors.

She did not.

She turned, watching as he clomped awkwardly through the snow to the end of the haphazardly shoveled flagstone walkway. He stopped at the rock pillar which held the low, black wrought iron gate, more decorative than useful, and thinking that after putting his foot in it, the least he could do was to give her some distance.

"I'm sorry." His breath crystallized as he spoke. "I didn't—"

"Know," she finished for him. "Yeah. I figured." Her shoulders rose as she pulled in a breath. Next, she'd be rolling them and loosening her neck like a fighter. Sean was not fooled. He'd struck a nerve and it had elicited a flight rather than fight response, and that meant he'd hurt her.

"I'm sorry," he repeated.

"You didn't do anything wrong, but if it helps, apology accepted." Her hair shifted across her back as she reached for the door handle, then her hand dropped to her side. "I owe you an apology, too."

"How so?"

One corner of her mouth tightened. "That thing where I said you weren't pretty."

"You were stating a fact."

"Tactlessly so." Her mouth tightened. "I work with the public. I generally hold my tongue better than that."

"But not with me?"

A better question would be why didn't he stop talking? He had intended to make amends, then head back to where Dillon was supposedly working, but more likely spying on them. Instead he was prolonging matters.

Maddie took a few steps toward the edge of the porch. "Maybe because you and I had that friction when we worked together." She spoke carefully, as if piecing together the reason for her tactlessness. "I guess I'm still feeling... I don't know—"

"Combative?"

She made a face. "Oh, yeah. I'm so combative."

She wasn't...but he could see it happening, which surprised him. Old Maddie would have never toed her way up to a fight.

Maddie brushed her hair back after the breeze lifted it. "I'm not myself."

It was a simple statement of fact and one he could identify with. He knew what it was like trying to find equilibrium during trying times.

"You're going through a rough patch, Maddie. You're going to do things out of character every now and again. Stress does that."

She tilted her head, giving him a "who are you?" look. He had to admit that she had a point, but he forged on. He, who never got too involved in anyone's personal affairs unless invited, said, "Here's the thing from one broken-engagement person to another. There are stages you go through, but it gets better." He glanced toward the barn, saw no sign of Dillon. "My advice is not to get hung up in the anger stage for too long."

"How long is too long?"

He had no solid answer for that. "Varies, I guess. You'll know if the anger starts coloring everything."

"Noted." She tucked a few strands of hair behind her ear. A rueful smile curved her lips. "So much for staying out of each other's personal business."

"This is a one-off," he assured her. "And if it helps, I don't need an apology." Her eyebrows came together in a questioning look, so he added the obvious. "Because I never was pretty."

She gave him a disbelieving look. "If you say so."

"No. Really."

She shook her head as if he'd just informed her that the world was flat, then pulled the lodge door open and disappeared inside, leaving him standing on the flagstone walk, wishing he'd kept his mouth shut about her apology.

Maddie found him attractive?

How else could he interpret what had just happened?

But there'd been no sign of attraction when they'd worked together, and Maddie had been an open book back then…or so he'd thought.

Could it be that optimistic waters ran deep?

As Sean headed to the barn, he shuffled through his memories of their time together. He'd thought she was cute, yet annoyingly out of touch with reality. She'd probably pegged him as some kind of curmudgeon. Cranky. Pessimistic.

They hadn't had a good relationship, so, if she'd found him attractive, it wasn't because he'd been charming.

"How'd she take it?"

Sean jumped when Dillon spoke from the dark corner where he sat on a straw bale.

"We're good." He wanted to ask who Maddie had been engaged to, but let the question slide. What did it matter, really? It was doubtful he knew the guy.

Dillon got off the bale. "Glad to hear it. The last thing we need is a lot of tension if we're going to survive the open house."

"Is the open house that bad?"

"It's all-consuming." He cocked his head. "Or at least it is when Mom is at the helm. Maybe we could be a little more laid-back?"

"Maybe." He really wasn't on board for all-consuming, but he'd do whatever he needed to in order to help out Max and Shirl.

"Mom will want photos."

"Probably."

"I'm pretty sure I can't use the ones from last year. She'd figure it out."

"I think she'd figure it out when someone asked her why Lucky Creek didn't participate."

"Yeah." Dillon kicked the loose straw on the floor in front of him. "I'm hosed."

"We're hosed," Sean said, planting a hand on the teen's shoulder.

Dillon grinned. "Guess I'll show you guys where the stuff is later today. There's a lot, and we should probably get a plan in place."

"We have one. I'll check fences."

"Nice try." Dillon put on his serious face. "I'll tour you guys through before I go to practice today. Then you'll see what we're up against."

Don't hold on to the anger for too long.

Good advice.

Excellent advice.

Except Maddie wasn't at the anger phase. She was in the "how did this happen" phase.

The "going through the motions of life while waiting for the brain fog to lift" phase. The "how can I ever trust my instincts again" phase. She'd believed that she and Cody would be happy for the rest of their days with a certainty that hadn't allowed for doubts, and therefore ignored what she hadn't wanted to see. She'd pretended all was well and felt good doing it.

Looking back…sheesh. Talk about dodging reality. She was disappointed in herself for not looking at things more critically; for hanging on to the "everything will work out" mindset.

Things had worked out—but not in a good way.

She pinched the bridge of her nose. She was turning into Sean.

And, while she was on the subject, was it possible that the man whose smoldering good looks had inspired many a rodeo groupie, and made him the perfect spokesperson for Rodeo Denim, had no idea just how attractive he was, scar or no scar? Because despite her impulsive comment about not being pretty, he was still ridiculously attractive—just in a more worn-around-the-edges way.

"Hey, Maddie?" Dillon's voice rang through the lodge hall.

"Kitchen," she called. A few seconds later he wandered in dressed in insulated overalls and carrying his bright green jacket.

"Do you need one of us to go with you when you take your stuff to the Farley Ranch?"

"I can handle it. At least one of the brothers should be there."

"Cool. I'm going with Sean to look at the fences. He wanted to go on horseback, but I talked him into taking the snowmobiles."

"Good plan."

"Someone needs to keep an eye on him," Dillon added, patting his leg. "My dad told me that Sean gets stubborn and that he might get in over his head trying to do everything he used to do before he was ready."

"Your dad is a wise man."

"And he's known Sean for a long time."

"Do you think you can stop him if he decides to do something?" Maddie asked with genuine curiosity.

JEANNIE WATT

"Nope. But I can help sweep up the pieces."

"Ouch." Maddie made a face, but Dillon just laughed.

"Kidding. I'll keep him out of trouble."

"Good luck."

Dillon touched his forefinger to the brim of his winter hat, then disappeared back into the hall. A moment later Maddie heard one of the double doors open and then Dillon called, "We're clear."

The door shut, leaving Maddie to wonder who had helped sweep up the pieces after Sean had been injured this last time. He appeared to be very much alone, and, reading his vibe, which rolled off him in waves, he liked things that way. That worked because the only person that she really needed to have a normal relationship with on this ranch was Dillon. She and Sean would coexist. Like he'd said, his apology and the conversation that followed was a one-off. They knew where they stood with one another and now they could retreat to neutral corners.

She pushed off the table and rolled her

shoulders. Life would have been a whole lot simpler had it just been she and Dillon on the Lucky Creek Guest Ranch. But that wasn't the case, and while she no longer believed that things would work out in the end, she did believe that this, too, would pass.

Her phone, which she'd left on after sending "I'm doing okay" texts to Whit and Kat that morning, buzzed.

Cody.

This, too, will pass

She resisted the urge to silence the phone in case Dillon wasn't able to keep Sean out of trouble while they checked fences—or vice versa—and crossed the kitchen to the coffeepot, tamping down an emotion that was beginning to feel more like anger than sorrow. She and Cody had spoken three times since the breakup to discuss the necessary details of canceling a wedding. Each time had left her shaken, and now he needed to leave her alone. The wedding was canceled, the guests notified and the vendors had pocketed their deposits. It was done. *Fini.*

Maddie closed her eyes.

This is your new reality. Embrace it. Move on.

It would be a whole lot easier to do that if Cody would stop calling.

"THE FENCES ARE in stupidly good shape," Dillon muttered after they'd made their last stop at the far end of the winter pasture.

Riding through the snow, bouncing over drifts, feeling the spray of crystals hitting his goggles, Sean felt alive in a way he hadn't in a very long time. He needed more time in the open air, so in that respect well-maintained fences were a disappointment. He'd have to find another project to keep him busy between feeding and maintaining the waterers in subzero temperatures.

"Maybe the coach will have extra practices and you can get out of open house prep," he said.

"I don't shirk my duty."

Dillon stood looking out over the pastures that would one day be his and Sean wondered if the kid realized how fortunate he was to have his future secured. To know that no matter what, he had a place to land.

He didn't know if he was an easy read, or if it was coincidence that Dillon turned to him to ask, "What are you going to do after the holidays? After you leave here, I mean. Will you stay in the area?"

"I don't know," Sean said matter-of-factly.

"Dad would probably hire you, you know, if you needed a place to work."

Sean pushed the thumbs of his gloved hands into the pockets of his Carhartt jacket. He wouldn't mind ranch work, but he wasn't up to dealing with guests for another summer, which was why he'd only lasted one season the last time he'd worked for Max.

"Actually, I've applied to some schools and training programs."

Dillon perked up. "What do you want to be?"

"When I grow up?" Sean asked wryly. Dillon nodded, ignoring the irony in Sean's voice. "I'm looking at diesel mechanics, which was what I'd intended to do after high school. The best programs are full up, but I'm on the wait list for my preferred school. I'll start next January."

Dillon let out a low whistle. "Long time."

"It is." He hadn't given the future a lot of thought while he'd been riding because he had a healthy bank account, and he was winning, so, like that stupid grasshopper in the story, he'd put off thinking about the lean times. He'd always felt that he had time to make decisions about a post-rodeo career. That things would work out.

Had Maddie's optimism rubbed off on him at some point?

No. He'd simply been arrogant.

It hadn't served him well, and suddenly he'd been faced with having to do something about his nebulous future; so he'd done what the guidance counselor in high school had suggested. He applied to mechanics programs. He'd always had a knack for repair, and he'd aced his automotive classes back in the day, but rodeo had kept him in a pretty small bubble. The tuition costs had been an eye-opener, as was the fact that the programs were so popular that it was difficult to secure a place.

He shot a look at Dillon. "What do you plan to do after you graduate?"

"I…" the teen twisted his mouth sideways as if expecting some pushback, "… I'm looking at teaching. Probably high school."

"Really?"

"My friends think it's a little lame, but I like working with people and I could coach wrestling."

"I don't think it's lame. Judging from my own experience as a student, I think teachers should get hazard pay."

Dillon laughed. "I agree."

"I guess we'd better get back," Sean said.

Dillon nodded, once again staring out at the pastures. "It's nice out here."

It was. The snow was deep, with just enough crust on it to catch the sunlight and reflect a zillion different colors, and the air was brisk, yet pleasant against his exposed skin.

"It'll be nice at the lodge, too, when you start walking us through the decoration thing."

"It will be," Dillon said in a bracing voice. "Totally." He made a face, then headed toward his snow machine, his boots cracking the sparkling crust of snow as he trudged along.

A few minutes later, as his snowmobile sailed over snow on the way back to the ranch, Sean debated about what he was going to do when he left the Lucky Creek Ranch. Mid-February would be there before he knew it, and he needed to find a job before then so as not to eat into his savings.

Yep. Time to do something he really hated, and make some calls.

MADDIE JUMPED WHEN her phone rang shortly after she'd returned from dropping her belongings at the Farley Ranch. She muttered a few exasperated words as it rang again.

This was *not* the way she was going to live her life, dodging things that hurt. She picked up the phone, ready to find out why Cody kept calling, only to find her business partner Kayla's name on the phone display.

Kayla she could deal with. That said, she

could also deal with Cody. And she would if he called again.

"Hey," she said in a voice that sounded falsely bright.

"Hi. I hope I caught you at a good time." Kayla spoke with just the right amount of concern mixed with I-know-you-have-this.

"It is. Is everything okay at the shop?"

"Fine. Elsa starts tomorrow and she's grateful for the hours, but not for the reason."

"I'm grateful she's there. I need a break from white lace and satin."

"Well, pink is the new color," Kayla said on a light note. And indeed, they had just received three blush wedding gown samples, following the latest trend. "I'm calling to make sure that you're doing okay."

"I am." As well as could be expected, anyway. "The lodge is a nice getaway." She saw no reason to mention that she didn't have the solitude she'd counted on.

"I'm also calling with some news."

Maddie couldn't say she liked the sound of that. "The good kind?"

"Danna Elliot moved up her wedding date."

Which wouldn't be a concern, except that Maddie, who'd taken basic fashion design classes along with her business courses, had promised to sketch some dresses and collaborate with the local miracle-working seamstress, Ashley Montgomery, to turn her ideas into a gown. Maddie and Ashley had collaborated a number of times, Frankensteining commercial sewing patterns together to make one-of-a-kind dresses—in Danna's case a cross between cowgirl queen and punk rock princess. It wasn't a service that Spurs and Veils offered, but when she had the time and inclination, Maddie volunteered. She'd known Danna since she was a child, so designing a one-of-a-kind punk cowgirl gown had sounded like a fun challenge. Little had she known...

"By a few days?" she asked hopefully.

"Two months. The venue they'd originally wanted has opened up and they can get out of the contracts for the other...long story short, the ceremony is now in May and Ashley needs a couple of months to make the dress. I know this is hard, and I didn't want to call, but—"

"It's fine."

It wasn't, but she would make it fine through strength of will. Maybe diving into a dress design would help her deal with her wedding PTSD.

Or make it worse. A lot worse.

Maddie's little voice was becoming remarkably snide, and she was having a hard time shutting it down. It was like she had to ride the full pendulum swing from optimism to pessimism before she could find a middle ground.

"Maddie, you don't have to do this. I can talk to Danna—"

"I'll get something to her in the next few weeks." She tried to sound businesslike, but had no idea if she'd pulled it off. The last thing she wanted to do was to design a wedding dress, but she'd made a commitment, and, unlike Cody, she would follow through.

"I'm sorry that my design abilities are nil, because you know I'd do this in a heartbeat." Her business partner's tone was warm and understanding causing Maddie's throat to tighten. Kayla cleared her own throat, before saying, "Do you want weekly status reports until you come back or—"

"After Christmas," Maddie said. "Unless there's another pressing issue, give me until then."

"Sure. If you need anything, anything at all—" Kayla's tone became firm, almost stern "—call. I mean it."

"Thanks, Kayla. I'll keep you in the dress design loop."

"And I'll tell Danna that you'll be in touch."

"Sounds good." Maddie ended the call and set her phone on the table, wondering if this was some kind of sign from the universe. If so, she didn't know what the message was.

Perhaps it was that she couldn't escape happy-ever-afters, even though she couldn't claim one of her own. She was destined to be a vicarious happy-ever-after-er.

The thought caused the corners of her mouth to tighten grimly. She'd take vicarious if it meant never being emotionally walloped again.

She picked up her teacup and carried it to the nearest sink where she rinsed it and then dried it with a crisp linen towel. The lodge boasted a huge kitchen with three sinks, one for prep, one for washing dishes and one just because, as near as Maddie could tell. When she'd worked on the ranch, the kitchen had actually seemed small as several people worked to prepare guest meals and special occasion dinners, but having a kitchen this size to herself... well, it was kind of a dream after working in the small trailer house kitchenette.

She caught a movement outside the window and saw Sean and Dillon heading from the equipment barn to the house. Dillon promised to show them where everything was stored before leaving for practice that day, and apparently the time was upon them.

The two men stomped on the mat outside the double doors, then came inside along with a gust of cold air. Dillon draped his coat over a chair, then rubbed his hands together.

"Cold out there. Something to do with it being December, I guess."

"How are the fences?" Maddie asked.

"According to my partner here," Sean indicated Dillon with a tilt of his head, "they are in stupidly good shape."

"It's true," Dillon said. "Which means that it's time to focus on Christmas." He pointed toward the door leading to the back of the lodge where the storage and staging areas were located. "Ready to see the treasures?"

"I am," Maddie said, noting that Sean didn't look particularly enthusiastic. It must have been a blow to have the fences all in good order. Not that he didn't have other things to take care of, but he didn't have enough to excuse him from decorating.

"Did you get your stuff dropped off at the Farley Ranch?" he asked as they followed Dillon to the storage area.

"I did. Kat's brothers helped me unload and everything is safely locked in the silo." Now all she had to do was to figure out where the stuff would land next. Where *she* would land next.

Dillon stopped in front of the storage room door. "We're behind schedule," he said. "Mom usually starts decorating the day after Thanksgiving. She'd start earlier, but my dad has some strong beliefs about when Christmas should begin and end. Anywho, this year, on my advice, she didn't decorate." He shot a dark look at them. "Then you two came along."

"Dillon, surely you don't hate—"

"I'm no Grinch," Dillon interrupted. "But there should be some kind of law against overdecorating."

Sean caught Maddie's eye and mouthed, *Grinch*.

Dillon made a growl low in his throat, then opened the storage room door and stepped back, giving Sean and Maddie a clear view of the packed interior. Row upon row of neatly labeled boxes lined the shelves.

"All this stuff goes up?"

"Thankfully, no. We change themes. This year the theme is 'Old-Fashioned

Christmas,' according to Mom, and she wants us to use the stuff in those shelves." He pointed to the east wall.

"It's still a lot," Maddie said as she ran her gaze over the floor-to-ceiling shelving unit.

"Oh, yeah," Dillon replied. "On a normal year, we hire someone to take everything down and store it away while we're in Mexico, but this year, I guess we get the honors there, too."

Maddie glanced at Sean. "I think this is a decent trade-off. A roof over our heads in exchange for putting on a holiday fete."

"Yes," Sean agreed. "A decent trade-off. What's a fete?"

"A shindig," Dillon muttered. He didn't sound convinced that it was a decent trade-off, but he was resigned. "It's not *that* bad, really. It's just…a lot."

Looking at the decorating task ahead of them, Maddie had to agree.

"Last year our open house made a national magazine because the editor was visiting family in the area and was so impressed with what Mom had done. That really spurred her on. We got a surge in reservations and two requests for winter weddings, which Mom turned down."

"Thankfully," Maddie murmured, earning a sideways look from Sean which she pretended not to notice. She'd never minded letting her emotions show, but this situation was different, and she felt a strong need to protect herself.

Do not offer sympathy, Sean. Not even a look. Just...don't.

Like he would.

But...he had apologized.

A moment later while Dillon was explaining the labeling system, which assured that everything went to the correct place in the storage room when they packed up again, Sean said in an undertone, "Are you okay?"

"Why do you ask?" Maddie's cheeks went warm as she spoke. She'd thought she'd been doing a good job hiding how much the idea of sketching a wedding dress was getting to her.

"No reason," he said in a way that made it clear he had reason.

"I'm fine. Just having Christmas flashbacks."

Sean gave her a quick frowning look, telling Maddie he hadn't accepted her flippant answer. Well, he could accept it or not. She didn't mind, because her business was none of his.

"Does anyone care if I tackle the outside stuff on my own?" he asked.

Dillon shook his head. "It's a team effort, man. We can start with the outside, but we're going full three musketeers. Trust me. It's easier that way."

"If you say so. Next question, when do we start?"

Dillon pulled out his phone and brought up the calendar, holding the phone so that both Sean and Maddie could see the screen.

"We're here." His finger hovered over the calendar. "The open house is here." He pointed at December 16.

"A little over two weeks from now?" Sean stuffed his hands in his rear pockets as he craned his neck to see without moving closer to Maddie. "Plenty of time to get ready."

"I wish. The photographer comes here."
Dillon planted his finger on December 6.

"Photographer?" Maddie and Sean spoke
in unison. Dillon answered with a grim nod.

"The local paper runs ads for the event.
We need to be ready."

"Which gives us not that long," Sean said.

"And since I'm in school…" Dillon wag-
gled his eyebrows, "…you guys are going
to be busy."

"Team effort, man," Sean said, putting a
hand on Dillon's shoulder and giving him
an encouraging squeeze. "Maddie and I
will take care of the other pressing issues
while you're at school."

"And wrestling practice."

"He has a point," she said. For all of his
talk about team efforts, he wasn't going to
be there to referee or act as a nice protective buffer during a good part of the work-
day. She told herself that they didn't need a
buffer. Sean would provide that by simply
being himself.

"I'm not backing out," Dillon said. "I'm
saying that we can get it all done this com-

ing weekend. It'll be a couple of full days, but yeah. Doable."

Maddie ran her gaze over the storage unit crammed with bins, then met Sean's gaze. "Doable," she said solemnly.

The corner of Sean's mouth twitched. "So the young man says."

Maddie bit her lip to keep from smiling at the unexpected moment of connection... but biting her lip did not keep a warm feeling from unfurling inside of her as she held a sexy blue gaze; an unexpected and surprising warmth that was totally out of place given her current situation.

As if she didn't have enough to deal with.

CHAPTER FIVE

"THANKS, FINN. If you hear of anything else, let me know." Sean shifted his phone to the other ear as he pushed open the cabin door and stepped inside after knocking the snow off his boots and brushing off the shoulders of his coat. A small flurry had blown through as he'd fed the cattle that morning, but now the sun was breaking through

"I'll keep my ear to the ground, buddy. Glad to hear that the leg is coming along. It'll open things up more."

Finn Dawson, Sean's former rodeo travel partner, was now something of an agribusiness jack-of-all-trades. He sold ranch insurance policies, had a farm auction business and, in his spare time, he and his dad ran a farm and ranch job site, helping pair up workers to open positions for a fee. Sean hoped, with his friend's professional help, he'd have another job lined up by the time the Tidwells returned to the Lucky Creek Ranch. There was nothing spectacular on the horizon jobwise, but Finn knew of a ranch in northern Wyoming looking for temporary hands during calving season.

Sean was willing to spend long nights in freezing temperatures, but he was hoping for a job that would last until he started diesel school in a year. Unfortunately, his insistence on being up-front about quitting after twelve months was not helpful to his job search. Nobody was looking for a one-year employee, which meant that he'd probably end up bouncing from one temporary job to another, which was fine, as long as he could keep finding temporary jobs. He did not want to touch his nest egg, which would just cover his training and living expenses until he hit the job market after completing his course of study. He fully expected his bank account to be approaching zero by that time, but he'd have a profession, which he lacked now.

Sean sat in one of the ridiculously comfortable buffalo plaid armchairs that flanked the propane-fueled potbelly stove in his cabin, and eased his feet out of his snow pacs. The heavy boots fell sideways as his feet came free. He scooted them aside, then grimaced as he stretched out his aching leg. His knee popped and his thigh muscles howled. Sean let his head fall back against the chair cushion.

He'd known more than one rodeo rider who had become dependent on high strength painkillers and because of that, had weaned himself from all pain relievers except ibuprofen, which he avoided taking as much as possible. That said, a day spent slogging through the snow, fixing a frozen waterer, shoveling paths, and moving hay to areas where cattle and horses were fed had taxed his healing body.

He glanced at the bottle sitting on the small oak table near the window, then back at the stove.

Not yet. Let the heat do its work.

He was determined to muscle through as much as he could without drugs that relieved the pain, but messed with other parts of his body, like his stomach. Ice. Heat. Rest. Scratch the rest part. He wasn't good at it.

He settled more deeply into the armchair as the propane heat radiating from the cast-iron stove warmed his chilled body. He should have said yes when Maddie dutifully offered to help with outdoor chores after Dillon had left for school that morning, but he hadn't. Alone time seemed better, especially when he kept reliving the emotional kick he'd felt when he and Maddie had shared that brief moment of connection the previous day when Dillon had shown them the Christmas storage room.

It had been nothing. Literally nothing.

But the way she'd met his gaze as if they shared a secret made him *want* to share secrets with her and that felt threatening. A jilted bride and a washed-up bronc rider, both licking their wounds and certain to go their separate ways in a matter of weeks, didn't need to add another complication to their lives—and he had the strong and unwelcome feeling that if he didn't watch himself things could get complicated. This new Maddie intrigued him, and he was not in a position to be intrigued.

His life had never been all that settled

or sane, but at least he'd had a career and an income. Now he had neither. He would have taken a beating rather than admit it, but as irritating as her proselytizing had been back in the day, he'd also been grudgingly charmed by Maddie's sweetness and optimism—and also convinced that they were from different planets. There'd been no middle ground between them…but now it seemed that there was.

That was where his sense of threat came from. The middle ground.

They'd agreed to stay out of each other's business the night they'd arrived, and so far, they'd pretty much failed at that.

He was going to have to up his game.

MADDIE'S HEART WAS not in wedding dress design—not even a cool punk-cowgirl-princess dress which was her jam. Whit had suggested that she back out of the project during their last exchange of texts, but she'd forged ahead, hoping that she'd be able to approach the project in a do-your-job way and then get caught up in the process. It wasn't working. She wasn't crying onto the paper or anything, but her creativity seemed to have left the building.

She put a couple more lines on a design that involved a cliché corset over miles of tulle, then crumpled it up and tossed it into the open kitchen waste can three feet away from the table where she worked. She'd made every shot that afternoon, which was unusual. Sometimes the floor of the trailer she'd rented from Cody's aunt and uncle looked like a paper recycling center.

But usually the stuff she threw away looked better than the designs she was trash canning today.

Frustrated, she pushed the sketch pad across the table, out of reach, and leaned back in the kitchen chair in the way her teachers warned kids not to, with the front legs dangling in the air. She almost went over when the door opened behind her. Dillon was at school, so that meant…

She righted the chair and coolly glanced over her shoulder at Sean Arteaga, ignoring the irritating way her heart rate bumped up at the sight of him. He brushed snow off his coat, then stepped inside, closing the door behind him.

"It's snowing again. I hope the kid makes it home all right."

"I'm sure he's made the drive in the snow before." It touched her that Sean was concerned. No...it was the fact that he'd mentioned his concern. Mr. Closed Book had never done anything like that when they'd worked together on the trail rides; not even when the twelve-year-old twin sisters had "borrowed" horses for an unsanctioned excursion into the mountains. He'd been plenty worried about finding them before sundown, as had she, but he hadn't said a word. Just kept his worry to himself, leaving Maddie to assure him that everything would be okay.

Which was almost certainly why he hadn't said anything.

Well, they were both changing. She was talking less. He was talking more. But they didn't really have much to say to one another, and that wasn't a bad thing.

Sean blew that theory out of the water a moment later when he pulled out a chair, sat himself down and said, "I think we should talk."

"You're scaring me."

He gave her a look. "I want to talk about the next few weeks. Christmas decorations. Open house. That stuff."

"Oh." Maddie grimaced. "When a person says, 'let's talk,' it's usually personal in some way."

"I don't do personal." The reply was automatic, spoken as his gaze strayed to the sketch pad. "Are you an artist?"

"No," she said with a touch of weariness. "I am a woman who agreed to design a wedding dress a few weeks ago, and now has to follow through on my promise."

"Ouch."

Her eyebrows lifted at the empathy conveyed in a single word by a man who "didn't do personal."

"I only design for certain clients. It's not my calling or anything. I've done it two or three times. Three. Yes. Three."

Was she babbling? It felt like she was. She cleared her throat, hoping the action would also clear her head.

"Maybe you should bow out this time?" he asked. "Circumstances and all."

"I have a business and a business partner to consider."

"But if this isn't a normal service..."

"I babysat this girl when I was in high school. She asked, and I said yes. It's a commitment."

"Surely she'd understand that your creativity has taken a hit."

"It has, but I'm all about getting back on the horse." She faked a cough. "Of course, first I have to *catch* that horse."

"You do," Sean agreed.

And it sure seemed like they were edging toward personal.

"Before we get too far afield," Maddie said, "what exactly do we need to talk about?"

"Division of duty."

"I'm happy to help with the outdoor chores when Dillon's at school. I told you—"

"Not that kind of duty. I don't mind taking care of that stuff alone. It gives me time to think."

"That's not always a good thing." She for one was getting very tired of thoughts circling through her head. Sad thoughts. Weary thoughts.

"The sting wears off with time."

Again. Unexpected empathy, which she could live with as long as she kept herself from believing that it was anything other than one survivor talking to another. "I think I owe you."

"For…?"

"Not being all sunny and positive and upbeat with me. Like I was with you. And Bill Connors when he got all those college rejections." The thought of Sean acting like that made her want to smile, albeit grimly.

"Yeah. I figured that you learned your lesson there." He rubbed a hand over his scarred cheek. Funny how the scar had changed his face, but had not made it less attractive.

"I was nineteen and figuring things out. I really believed what I was spouting."

He dropped his hand. "I hope you still do…a little, anyway." The admission appeared to surprise him, and he shifted in his chair. "Back to the division of labor. I've been thinking about this and looking at the pictures Dillon showed us, there's a lot of ladder work."

"And you're not a ladder guy right now."

"My leg is undependable," he admitted.

"You're not the only person who can go up a ladder, you know."

"I want to do my fair share."

"There's plenty to be done at ground level," Maddie said patiently. "You can put out all those angels."

She had to fight not to laugh at his expression.

"I'll do the train." The photos had shown a train circling the room, loaded with elves and presents.

"*And* the angels." She spoke with mock sternness.

"My leg is feeling better." He tapped his fingers on the table, then said, "Outside is almost all ladder stuff and I don't want you and Dillon to have to do it all. I was thinking of hiring someone—"

"No." His eyebrows lifted, and Maddie shrugged.

"Who put you in charge?" he asked, echoing her words from a few days ago.

"Max. You were out of the room, and he said, 'Maddie, you're in charge.'"

"Uh-huh," Sean said flatly.

"It's true."

Before Sean could answer, the double doors in the main lodge hall opened, and Dillon clomped into the house as only a teenage boy could. A second later he walked into the kitchen, gave a quick "hello" and headed straight for the refrigerator where he drank milk from the carton, then wiped his mouth with the back of his hand.

"Don't tell Mom, and use the other carton." He nodded at the unopened one behind the one he'd just drank out of. "Habit. I'm the only one that drinks milk when the parents are here, so…" His eyebrows came together as he spotted the sketch pad.

"Master plan?"

"Wedding dress designs for a client."

"I thought you were on vacay from the place."

Maddie shrugged. "Old friend. Special circumstances."

Dillon pulled up a chair, set the milk carton on the table and reached for the book, flipping open the cover. "Not a lot to see."

"Because it's all in there." Maddie jerked her chin toward the trash can. "Maybe tomorrow something will come to me." She held out a hand for the book and Dillon handed it to her.

"Should you be designing wedding dresses?" Dillon asked candidly. "I mean, you know...doesn't it kind of hurt?"

"Like a beast," Maddie admitted. Funny how when Dillon discussed the matter, she didn't feel as defensive as when Sean did.

Sean met her gaze and she guessed that he was thinking the exact same thing. So what?

"Actually, it's getting easier," she said, even though it wasn't, "but I've yet to come up with a decent idea." She pushed her chair back. "I'm going to start putting stuff out tomorrow while you're in school. It'll give me something to do. I'll just follow the photos in your mom's album."

"Okay," Dillon said slowly, as if loath to abandon his three musketeer plan.

"There'll be plenty to do this weekend,"

Sean added. "We can do the outside work and I'm not much use on a ladder, so you'll be taking point on that."

Dillon glanced at Sean's leg, then nodded. "I guess I will, so yeah. You setting stuff out in the house would put us ahead of the game. We can tweak before the photographer comes…yeah. Sounds good."

"Did you eat?" Maddie asked.

"Wrestlers don't eat."

"This one is going to," Sean said in something approaching a dad voice.

Dillon pushed his chair back. "I'll probably blow my weight class, but fine. I'll eat."

"And I'm going to my room to make some calls," Maddie said, even though she had exactly zero calls to make. Instead she was escaping proximity to a man who both attracted and confused her. It wasn't like she could escape for long, but she needed time to center herself and figure out what was going on.

She'd been weeks away from being a bride—a bride who'd had no second thoughts—and she had no business being so aware of a guy she hadn't seen in forever. A guy who didn't really like her all that much. He might like her more now that she'd dropped the sunny disposition, but Sean Arteaga was a loner, and she was a temporary loner.

So…maybe she was simply attracted to the one thing they had in common—a need to be alone.

Yes.

Maddie decided to grab hold of that theory and hang on tight.

"Do you think she's okay?" Dillon asked in a low voice.

The sound of Maddie's footsteps grew fainter as she walked down the hall leading from the kitchen to the staff bedrooms. Sean waited for the bedroom door to open and close before he said, "I think so." Then he off-handedly changed the subject. "How was practice?"

"Sweaty." Dillon leaned sideways to make certain that Maddie was actually in her room, then said, "I don't think she should be doing wedding stuff, what with…you know."

"If she's doing it, I guess it's something

she needs to do." But Sean was fairly certain that Maddie would have preferred not to be deep diving into anything that reminded her of her own canceled nuptials, just like he now avoided rodeo. Not because of bitterness or anything—just because it hurt to accept that his career was gone, and he hadn't chosen to leave. The choice had been made for him. The same thing had happened to Maddie.

"Who was Maddie going to marry?" He'd told himself a dozen times not to ask, but here he was. Asking.

"Cody Marsing."

"There's a Marsing Ranch east of Larkspur, right?" Sean grew up in a town on the other side of the mountain range, and didn't know that many Larkspur locals, but he knew the ranches.

"Right. Cody's a good guy, really." Dillon's expression became thoughtful. "Except for the part about him dumping Maddie." He took hold of the milk carton as it sat on the table, making no move to lift it. "But what do I know?" He gave Sean an easy smile, making Sean wish that he could tap into the kid's laid-back personality. Where was the teenage angst?

Dillon lifted the carton, drank, then set it back on the table. They sat in silence, then the teen cocked his head, as if a thought had just occurred to him. "Do you know Cody?" he asked.

"No. I wondered if I might, but I didn't want to ask Maddie the guy's name."

"Protective instincts kicking in."

Dillon was unnervingly astute for a kid his age. Sean didn't protest, because of that thing Shakespeare said. Protesting would only fine-tune the kid's radar.

"A dumped bride makes a guy feel protective," Dillon continued blithely. "Nothing wrong with that."

Nothing at all, as long as he kept it at that.

"Where are the schools you applied to?" Dillon shifted subjects abruptly, but Sean didn't think it was because the kid sensed that Sean wanted to talk about something other than the topic he himself had brought up.

"One's in Wyoming, the other in eastern Montana. It's weird to think about going to school at my age." Even though lots of guys his age did it.

"Would you change the past if you could? I mean...would you have gone to diesel school right out of high school instead of doing the rodeo thing?"

"No," Sean said slowly. He'd be in better shape physically if he'd ditched rodeo early on. And there was no doubt that he'd messed up two decent relationships due to his career choice, but being a bronc rider had defined him. Made him who he was in many ways. He wouldn't have given that up.

But that didn't keep him from leveling a hard look at Dillon. "But I would be in better shape if I had given up rodeo. Stay. In. School."

Dillon grinned. "I don't have anything cool to distract me like a bronc riding career, so yeah. I have every intention of staying in school."

DECORATING THE MAIN hall of the lodge was going to take more time than Maddie had anticipated—mainly because her coworkers were spending more time playing with the train set than attending to other matters, such as angel placement. She and Sean had spent the afternoon pulling out the appropriate boxes and studying photographs, but they hadn't gotten much of a start by the time Dillon arrive home from school.

"Trust me on this," Dillon said as he took the train control from Sean. "If you put Santa in the first car, it can't make that sharp corner by the lamp."

Sean took a hard look at the track, then back at the car where he'd placed Santa.

"Maybe if we tweak the angle just a tad…"

Dillon shook his head. "I have tweaked. Santa is supposed to ride in that car, but he's never done so successfully due to the setup. Now, if I could talk Mom into moving the sofa and end table so that the tracks can lay there—" he pointed at the sofa leg "—but no. Something about the symmetry of the room…"

Maddie headed to the storage closet to put an empty bin back in its spot and then returned to the main hall in time to see Santa take a spill on the corner.

"See?" Dillon said, while Sean rubbed the back of his head. "But if he's in the last car, it works. Go figure."

"Huh." Sean set his hands on his hips as he studied angles. "There's got to be a way—"

Maddie cleared her throat, and both looked her way.

"Right," Sean said, correctly reading her "let's do this" expression.

Dillon made a guilty face as he put the train cars back on the track, setting Santa in the last one. "Angels," he said.

Shirl had created a wonderful suite of decorations for her Old-Fashioned Christmas theme. An antique hobbyhorse with a holly wreath around its neck was placed next to the empty spot where the tree would stand. Other antique toys—nutcrackers, teddy bears, the train set—were tastefully arranged throughout the high-ceilinged room. Eventually fairy lights would twinkle around the window casements—tomorrow's task—and candles would be arranged on the tables amidst evergreen bows and antique glass ornaments.

And that was only the main hall.

The bathrooms, the dining area and even the kitchen would also be decorated, along with doors and hallways. When she commented aloud about how much there was to do, Dillon gave her an I-told-you look.

"Then we get to start outdoors this weekend," he said.

Maddie only hoped they were done with the house by then. The boughs, wreaths and trees, as in plural, would be delivered the next day, and Maddie planned to use the time while Dillon was at school and wrestling practice to set those up and get a head start on decorating.

Then they would start lighting the outside, which according to Dillon, was the most time-consuming part of the "ordeal" as he called it.

"We have to wrap each newel post for the full effect."

"Ah," Maddie and Sean had said in unison when he'd explained.

"Then light the outside trees, string the

lights along the eaves, and put up the snow-men and the Nativity scene."

It sounded garish, but Maddie knew from the photos that it was not. Shirl had a deft hand and while a lot of the property was lit up, it was with small twinkly lights, more delicate than glaring.

"And then, of course, the sleigh."

"What sleigh?" Once again Maddie and Sean spoke in unison before exchanging glances.

"The sleigh in the barn. It's half normal size and kind of rickety, but it looks cool. We haul it out, load it with fake presents, wrap the sticky out things with garlands."

"The sticky out things? The shafts?" Sean asked.

"Exactly."

"I didn't see that in the photos," Maddie said.

"It sits next to main gate. We put a big wreath on the gate, too. The pictures are at the back of the photo album."

Maddie went to the dining table and opened the album. Sure enough, on the last pages, past the sections for Cowboy Christmas, Country Christmas and Toyland Christmas, were two pages showing the ranch entrance with a big wreath and the sleigh next to it.

"We do the main gate the same every year, so Mom doesn't have those photos in the other sections."

"Which theme do you like best?" Maddie asked, flipping back through the pages.

"Toyland. They did that one for me when I was a little guy, and I had a blast picking out the stuff. I make them set up the train every year now."

"Wise," Sean said. "We're going to figure out that Santa problem."

"Can't be done unless we change the angle at the end table..."

Maddie headed back to the dining table where she pulled out the lights that would be mounted around the window casings the next day.

"I thought we were leaving those for tomorrow," Sean said from where he was working on the train.

"I'm prepping."

"For..."

Maddie pulled the last string out of its box, laying it on the table next to its mates, ready to plug in and test. "When Kayla and I decorate the shop, we lay everything out, make sure the lights work, then we start. Saves some heartache later." And she'd always enjoyed decorating the shop, which they'd planned to do the evening after Thanksgiving. Kayla and Elsa had handled the job without her this year, and she'd been happy to let them do it.

"Smart," Sean said a second before the phone buzzed in his pocket. He pulled it out, glanced at the screen, then said, "I need to answer this."

"I'll handle the track while you're gone," Dillon said to Sean before shifting his attention to Maddie. "If I move the sofa everything will be cool.

"Symmetry," she reminded the teen with a grin as Sean took a couple of steps toward the hall leading to her and Dillon's rooms, stopped and said hello. He stood with his head cocked to one side, listening intently as both she and Dillon made a show of not paying attention to him.

"I'll hear him out," Sean finally said, "but it's not—no, you're right. Sure."

Curiosity niggled at her as she plugged in one end of an extension cord to test the lights. She knew full well that Sean's business was none of hers, but, given his injuries and what she assumed was an uncertain future, she couldn't help but wonder who he would hear out. A potential employer, perhaps?

Why do you care?

It was a reasonable question; one she'd answered the night before when she found herself wondering why a guy that she hadn't seen for ten years kept pushing his way into her brain.

Her conclusion was that their summer of butting heads had created a bond. She'd had the same experience when she'd attended a horsemanship camp as a young teen and the only person that she'd known there was a girl she hadn't gotten along with at school. They'd been the youngest participants, occasionally on the receiving end of some mild bullying, and intimidation had gone a long way toward helping them form a bond. Now she and Whitney Fox were the best of friends, almost as close as sisters.

Which made her wonder—were she and Sean on their way to becoming friends?

She tried to picture that. Couldn't do it.

But she could picture other things. More intimate things inspired by his physicality that were never going to happen. All the same, she was glad that she had a decent poker face.

He turned then, phone still in his hand, caught her mid-stare, and she jerked her gaze away.

So much for poker face.

But if there was a silver lining, and her former self would have insisted that there was, it was that having Sean around did a decent job of distracting her from recent disappointments.

She'd take it.

AFTER HIS CALL, Sean and Dillon abandoned the train and focused on toting the remaining boxes of decorations from the storage room to the areas where he and Maddie would unpack them the next day. After the shelves were emptied and the boxes and bins distributed, with the outside decorations stacked near the front door, Dillon made a sandwich and retired to his room to study algebra. Maddie stood hands on hips in the middle of the lodge hall, surrounded by boxes and looking just this side of overwhelmed.

"And to think, I wasn't going to celebrate Christmas this year," she said more to herself than to him.

"Same here."

He came to stand next to her, pulling in a long breath as they silently surveyed the cluttered room. Tomorrow, most of the bins would be back in storage, but at the moment, chaos reigned.

Maddie shifted her weight, folding her arms over her chest, and he realized that he was very tuned in to her movements. Such an odd feeling, being drawn to a woman that he'd put off-limits in his head.

"Why wouldn't you celebrate Christmas?"

She turned her head slowly, meeting his gaze with an "I have to explain?" look.

"I understand the obvious reason," he said quickly. "But didn't you have plans? You know…before?"

She shook her head. "Cody and I would have celebrated with his aunt and uncle." She focused on the dimly lit yard on the other side of the bay windows. "Ain't going to do that now."

She spoke dryly, but he sensed the edge of pain. Understood it, too.

"Couldn't you go…" He was about to say, *home to family*, but stopped himself, realizing he actually knew next to nothing about her background.

"My grandparents are gone, and my dad is on the other side of the country, happily married to a woman I don't see eye to eye with. My visits are infrequent." She smiled a little without looking at him. "I think she thinks I take up too much of his time."

"That sucks."

"Doesn't it? But Dad and I talk, and I'm glad he's happy."

"What about your mom?"

Again the smile, but it drooped. "I lost her when I was really young."

He'd had no idea.

"You spend Christmas alone every year?"

She gave him a surprised look. "No. Before I started spending Christmas with my future aunt- and uncle-in-law, I spent the holidays with my friends' families. Either the Farleys, which was always an adventure, or the Foxes, which was less eventful, but always fun."

He realized he was staring and so did she.

"I have very little in the way of family," she said. "Aren't you the same?"

"Yes," he confessed. "It's just that... I didn't know you were so alone in the world."

"I'm not," she said simply. "Even though it kind of feels like it at times. Friends are as good as family. Maybe better because I get to pick them."

He gave a slow nod at the logic, and then after an awkward beat of silence, realized that they'd been standing in the same place for a little bit too long, almost as if neither of them was ready to make a move...or part company.

He turned to face her, mirroring her

folded arm stance, wondering if he was connecting with her or protecting himself. "You were so sunny that I just assumed you came from the classic nuclear family situation."

"I didn't." She gave him a challenging look. "But you did…before the accident. Right?"

"I did," he said. "We…" he didn't know how to finish. "We had a good life," he finally said. "Right up until Dad's heart attack. Mom had her own health issues and I think she kind of gave up after dad passed away." He ran a light hand over his scar. "Losing them so close together was…" He dropped his hand and met her gaze. "It's something I don't talk about. I like to remember them and the times we had, but—"

"It's personal and you keep your private stuff private. I get it."

She looked away, but Sean had the feeling that she did get it. She understood the privacy angle, probably because she was dealing with it now, what with curious people no doubt wondering how she was handling the breakup.

She made a small noise in her throat, part laugh, part sigh. "When I went to work at the bridal shop those few days before I decided to hide out, I felt like I had a neon sign blinking on my forehead that read, 'Dumped.'"

"Ouch."

"Yeah." She met his gaze again. "I felt naked. Stupid. And what's more," she added dryly, "I couldn't come up with a single silver lining."

"How about bullet dodged?"

"That one occurred to me, but it didn't make me feel any better." She made a face. "Everybody kept looking at me and pretending they weren't."

He rubbed his face, a habit he'd started during the healing process, and needed to stop. "Welcome to my world."

"Does it hurt?" she asked.

He didn't know what kind of hurt she was referring to, but he gave an honest reply that covered all bases. "A little. But the physical pain never bothered me as much as... I don't know...unspoken sympathy? I hate people feeling sorry for me. I'm no fan of being stared at either."

"You're right. That stinks."

"Even when I was doing the ad campaigns, I hated being the center of attention, but once the photo shoot was over, then the staring was over, and I could relax again."

"Was it strange seeing yourself on a billboard?"

"You have no idea, but," he said, rubbing his thumb and forefinger together, "it gave me a very nice bank account."

"Huh." She dropped the arms she'd kept protectively covering her chest.

"Huh what?" he asked curiously.

"I thought you were an attention junkie."

"Me?" He pointed at his chest.

"Not here at the ranch, when we were working together, but your profession put you in the public eye, and there were the magazine ads, and the billboard in downtown Missoula, and… I don't know what else. I thought you liked the attention of the crowd."

He gave a choked laugh. "No. I hate being looked at." His hand started to rise to his cheek, but he stopped it, unwilling to say that he hated it even more now, but that was the truth. It wasn't that he was mourning his loss of "prettiness" as Maddie had called it, but rather the unspoken sympathy in conjunction with a natural reticence. Turning up the charm to make his living was a skill he'd learned early on, and he was good at it, but he'd never felt natural doing it.

"Performing was one thing," he finally said, "because it was me against the bronc. It was a contest. But the autographs and stuff...killer."

He shifted his weight, wishing that Maddie wasn't looking at him like he was from Mars or some other faraway planet. "Thought you had me all figured out?"

"Maybe I didn't think about you at all."

Something in her tone didn't ring true.

"I'll tell you something I've never told anyone." The words kept coming, and he didn't try to stop them. She lifted her eyebrows in a skeptical expression, and he said, "It got worse toward the end."

"What did?"

"Anxiety, I guess. I loved riding broncs. Hated the public stuff."

"Let me get this straight. You didn't mind getting smashed into the dirt, but you didn't want to sign autographs?"

He shrugged his agreement. Funny how he was able to tell her something he'd barely admitted to himself, but it felt good saying the words aloud. "I guess that makes me a wimp?"

"Do you care if you're a wimp?"

His face relaxed into a smile that pulled at his scarred cheek. "No."

The clatter in the hallway made them jump, and also made Sean realize just how close they'd been standing after they'd dropped their protective folded-arm stances. When they turned to see Dillon picking up the plate he'd dropped on his way from his bedroom to the kitchen, he said, "Don't worry. I didn't see anything."

"If you did, I'd be concerned about your eyesight," Maddie said smoothly.

"Right," Dillon said, his cheeks a touch redder than usual. "Uh…tomorrow I won't be home until six o'clock. Just got a text from coach."

"That's fine," Sean said. "The team will carry on without you."

The team being he and Maddie, whose matter-of-fact attitude had probably been hiding under her sunny exterior back when they'd worked together. And he wondered if it was ultimately a good thing or bad that he hadn't caught a glimpse of who she really was back then.

CHAPTER SIX

"YOU DON'T HAVE to do this, Maddie." Danna Elliot spoke with the directness of an old friend. "It's an imposition, with us moving the wedding timetable up two months, and...well..." Her voice trailed as she refrained from stating the obvious. Maddie might not feel like designing a wedding dress when her own wedding had been canceled. "My sister's dress is gorgeous and with a few tweaks, no one will ever guess—"

"Danna, I'm good," Maddie said simply. "I've sketched a few ideas." She'd been restless the night before and stayed up watching a 1930s Christmas movie. The jolt of inspiration hit her while she watched Ginger Rogers's dress float around her as she masterfully outdanced her partner, who was not Fred Astaire. "I did the princess-punk-cowgirl design, plus a couple others that are retro and fun."

She'd sketched the retro designs first, then created the punk-princess-cowgirl design because that was what Danna had asked for. "Let me add some more detail and I'll drop them at Spurs and Veils for you to take a look. I'm going to town early next week if that works for you."

"It totally works and I'm very appreciative."

"It's my job." Maddie did not add, *And I love it*, like she might have before Cody put her world into a tailspin. She didn't love her job right now, but once she'd worked through the sense of loss and maybe the anger that Sean assured her was coming, she was sure she'd be happily steering brides to the perfect dress. Well…maybe not as happily as before because she was now questioning her beliefs.

She gave a little laugh, hoping to dispel any doubts Danna might still have. "On top of that, you're kind of special to me. Remember the mud pies?"

Danna laughed. "Oh, yes. You were the only babysitter who would indulge me."

"And you became a baker."

"Maybe we shouldn't tell people about the mud pies," Danna said with a laugh.

After Danna ended the call, Maddie stretched, then checked the clock. Almost six. Dillon was due back, and after he made one of his sandwiches, because he refused to let Maddie cook for him, the three of them would somehow maneuver the nine-foot-tall tree into the main hall and wrestle it into the gigantic stand that was already sitting in place near the stone fireplace.

And she'd finally see Sean, who'd been scarce that day, doing exactly what Max had asked him to do—handling mini-ranch emergencies. Another frozen waterer, a tractor that wouldn't start and, of course, the feeding, which he insisted on doing alone.

Maddie had skills in that regard, be it fixing tractors or feeding cows, and he knew she had skills, so if he chose to work alone, she wasn't going to beg for the opportunity to work by his side. While he'd been outside, battling the weather, waterers and tractors, she'd mounted the fairy lights around the windows and then continued working on dress designs for Danna, who'd then surprised her with a call.

"No Dillon?" Sean asked.

"He's probably driving slowly." It was snowing gently, but Maddie had checked the reports and the roads were plowed. And Dillon had assured her shortly after her arrival that he had been driving to and from the ranch for months, in all kinds of weather. He'd also told her with a wink that he'd really been driving for years, being a ranch kid, but now he was legal. In other words, the kid wasn't a novice snow driver, so yeah—probably a late practice.

Even so, Maddie kept an eye on the clock as she and Sean debated the best way to handle the tree. The consensus was with Dillon's help. Sean wasn't sure of his leg, and he was open about it. Maddie was strong, but she wasn't nine-foot-tree strong, so they decided to wait for Dillon, the muscle, to show up before dragging the monstrous evergreen into the lodge.

Dillon did not show up.

At seven o'clock, Sean said simply, "I'm going to look for him."

"I'll go with you." Maddie had spent the last forty-five minutes convincing herself that Dillon had a late practice, and that the cell reception was spotty if he hadn't thought to call before leaving town. But her stomach had slowly tightened as the minutes ticked by until it was now a hard knot of worry.

"Maybe you should stay here in case he shows up." Sean shrugged into his coat.

"I could do that. But I'm not going to."

He gave her a *Really?* look and she replied with a shrug. She might have stood back while he did the ranch work, but this was different. This was not a matter of getting alone time.

"Suit yourself."

They were just heading out the door when the headlights showed at the end of the driveway, arcing over the trees that flanked the entrance to the guest ranch.

"Those beams are too high for Dillon's little truck," Sean said as he came to a stop at the edge of the porch.

They were, and the way the truck dipped and bounced seemed familiar, very much like the way Cody's big one-ton Ford dipped and bounced when he drove across the unfinished parking lot behind Spurs and Veils to pick her up.

Maddie's stomach started to tighten.

Coincidence. There are a lot of Ford F-350s in the area.

But when the truck drove under the sodium light attached to the center bottom of the Welcome to Lucky Creek arch, she began to feel the now familiar numbness flood through her. That was Cody's rig, and there were two people in it.

Fight or flight?

That was her choice. The main door to the lodge was only a couple steps away, and Sean was more than capable of dealing with whatever situation was at hand.

Maddie pressed her lips together. *This is your new reality. You can embrace it, or you can run. Your choice.*

Another option was to stand in silence, not running, but not engaging, and ultimately that was the one she took.

Sean was almost to the gate when he realized she hadn't come with him. He glanced back, having no way of knowing why she held where she was, then continued on to meet the truck.

Dillon bailed out of the passenger side, carrying his gym bag and then, to Maddie's dismay, Cody shut off the headlights and opened his door. He dropped to the ground, but Dillon skirted the front of the truck, almost as if to head him off.

"Thanks for the ride, Cody. Appreciate it." He spoke quickly, as if he could hurry Cody on his way by talking fast.

Cody nodded at Dillon, who was not so casually blocking his path, then raised his gaze to Sean as he came to stand next to Dillon.

Was it her imagination, or were they forming a two-man cordon? Did Sean know who this was? She didn't see how.

"Sean Arteaga," he said to Cody without bothering to extend a hand.

"Cody Marsing. I've seen you ride."

"I had some car trouble," Dillon interjected. He didn't look at Maddie, as if by keeping his gaze on Cody, he could keep the man from noticing his ex-fiancée standing on the flagstone steps under the glow of an antique porch light.

Join them. Show him that he didn't shatter your world into a zillion razor-sharp pieces.

Maddie started down the steps, not allowing herself to think. Cody noticed the movement and then his chin came up when he recognized her. It was obvious from his response that he hadn't been aware she was living there.

"Cody," she said before he could speak, thus gaining a small mental advantage. She needed it. The man she'd thought she'd spend the rest of her life with stood five yards away, achingly familiar in some ways, and a stranger in others. It was the first time she'd seen him since the breakup, and her response was not what she'd expected. She felt...numb? Like she'd shoved the pain of the breakup so deep down that it wasn't able to surface easily.

A temporary thing, she was certain. After he left and she had some privacy, she'd probably feel all the emotions she wasn't allowing herself to feel now. Again, she'd take it. She would not break down in front of Sean and Dillon   or Cody for that matter.

"Maddie." Cody nodded, obviously off-balance by her unexpected presence. "I didn't know you were here."

She had the feeling that he was speaking to buy time as he regained equilibrium. "There's no reason you should," she replied coolly. Hurrah for feeling numb.

Cody's dark blond eyebrows came together under his felt hat as he considered her words. His good hat, she noted. He must be on his way to a function of some kind, although he could have been headed to the Marsing Ranch the long way, by highway, because of the snow.

"I swerved to miss a deer." Dillon took command of the conversation. "Hit a tree instead."

"Are you okay?" Maddie asked, automatically checking his face for bruises.

"It was a slo-mo kind of thing," Dillon said, and Cody nodded his agreement.

"Good thing he went the direction he did, or he would have wiped us both out." He pulled his gaze from Maddie's and focused on Sean, who he appeared to assume was a caretaker. "There's not too much damage to the truck. Dillon was going pretty slow when it happened."

"Bumper, grill and a stick through the radiator, thus the ride home." Dillon looked unhappy about that last part. Maddie put a hand on his shoulder and gave a squeeze through the thick wool of his letterman jacket.

Cody's gaze strayed to Maddie, and she could almost see the wheels turning in his head. He'd probably figured that she was on the Lucky Creek Ranch because of Max—she hadn't told his aunt and uncle where she was moving to, instead telling them that yes, she had a place to land— but he was probably wondering if the men flanking her on either side knew the story.

The fact that Sean eased half a step side-ways so that his arm pressed reassuringly against her shoulder might have answered the question, but...it also raised another. Was he being protective of her, or was she reading too much into the movement? Maybe he'd simply shifted his weight.

"I guess we'd better get the rig," Sean said to Dillon.

"I'll help you guys," Cody said. "It's on my way."

"Will you need me?" she asked Sean.

Before he could answer, Dillon said, "No. It's just a matter of pulling my truck back onto the road and towing it home." He looked at Cody. "Sean and I can handle it. I really appreciate the ride home. It would have been a long walk."

And then Cody was facing three expectant faces as Dillon, Sean and Maddie waited for him to get into his truck and drive away. When he turned toward his truck, a frisson of relief went through her, cutting through the numbness. She'd kept it together quite well, but for how long would she be able to do that?

"Sorry about that," Dillon said.

Maddie made a face at him, acting more casual than she felt for the kid's sake. "Like you had a lot of choice?"

"I didn't. It was either take the ride or walk.

I left my phone in my locker, and couldn't call—not that the phone would have helped because the accident happened in the dead zone—and I was really surprised that the other driver was...you know."

"The ex-fiancé who shall not be named?" Maddie asked, earning an appreciative smile from Dillon.

"Yeah," he said, looking relieved at her seemingly easy acceptance of what had just happened. He glanced over his shoulder as Cody got into his truck, then started the engine.

"Dillon," Maddie said, feeling the need to drive her point home. "I'm going to run into him. It was nice to have the first time be with friends by my side."

To prove her point, Maddie broke ranks and approached the driver's side of Cody's truck as the headlights came on.

"Why have you been calling me?" she asked when he rolled down his window, causing snow to fall off the ledge in little clumps.

"I had some questions about deposits, but Kayla helped me out."

"Great." She gave him a look that she hoped said, *Don't call again*.

"Maddie?"

She looked up to see Sean opening the door of Max's vintage GMC, which had lost more paint than it currently sported.

"Yeah. Coming." She met Cody's gaze, which was strangely blank, and realized that while the numbness was fading and her stomach was twisting into a knot, she felt more discomfort than sadness. Was it because he'd hurt her, destroyed her dreams and her utter reliance on the universe smiling on happy endings? Or was it something else, like, say, the realization that she'd dodged a bullet?

It was the first time the thought of dodging a bullet felt valid, but it was also one of the first days since the breakup that she didn't feel either numb or overwhelmed by sadness.

Nope. She felt angry.

Welcome, old friend. Anger felt much better than sadness. It felt empowering rather than demoralizing.

"Thank you for bringing Dillon home."

"Obviously that was not a problem. The kid was in trouble." He frowned at her. "Are you working here?"

"That's really none of your business." Sean had cautioned her not to let anger linger for too long. Fine. She wouldn't. But right now, faced off with Cody, she would indulge.

"I still worry."

"You don't get to."

He pushed his hat back as Maddie hugged her arms around herself. The cold cut through her MSU Bobcats hoodie, but she wasn't done yet. "Don't call me. Don't make contact. If there are any wedding issues, which I do not believe there are, you can leave a message at the shop."

He blinked at her, and she felt a twinge of satisfaction at having made her point. He'd ambushed her with a breakup; she was within her rights to demand that he leave her alone.

Sean started the truck he and Dillon sat in, the diesel engine knocking as it chugged to life, and Maddie took a step back from Cody's Ford.

Cody gave her a final look before starting the window glass rising again. Maddie turned and headed toward the house, not bothering to tell Sean and Dillon that she was not coming along.

As she started toward the lodge, she was struck by the very unsettling realization that she should be feeling stronger emotions. Maybe she couldn't attribute the odd numbness to shock. Maybe somewhere deep down, she knew that even though it stung, things had worked out for the best.

And maybe…it was hard to wrap her mind around the odd thought…but maybe, because of that, she owed Cody a debt of gratitude.

"IS SHE GOING to be all right?" Dillon craned his neck to watch Maddie disappear into the lodge as Sean swung the GMC in a backward arc.

"Yeah." He spoke as if certain, but that was mainly to make Dillon feel better. He obviously hadn't wanted to bring Maddie's worst nightmare onto the ranch, but the universe had had other plans.

"You sure?"

"Larkspur's a small town. They're going to run into each other."

"Yeah. She said that, but..."

Sean shot a look at the teen. "Not your fault. She's tough. Probably tougher than you and me." He didn't know why, but he believed it, even though his protective instincts were still in the process of standing down. He had nothing against Cody Marsing, but he found himself not wanting Maddie to have to deal with reminders of her broken engagement.

And what did that mean?

It means that you don't like to see people hurting.

He was going with that, even if it didn't feel like the whole truth. It was close enough for now.

"First of all, I couldn't believe that buck just walked out in front of me and stopped. Second, I can't believe that I hit a tree with a stub sticking out right at radiator level. I mean, what are the chances?"

"Did you go through a fence?"

"A little bit," Dillon said without looking at him. "Barbwire."

"That makes the chances pretty good, because the cows rub off the lower branches."

"I guess. But…" Dillon let out a breath. "The last thing I want to do is to hurt Maddie and I tried to get Cody to drop me at the gate, but he wouldn't, and I didn't want him to know that Maddie was there, because what if she didn't want him to know, and I didn't have my phone, 'cause I stupidly left it in my—"

"Take a breath," Sean said.

Dillon did, inhaling loudly, then blowing it out. "I wish it hadn't been him," he concluded.

"But it was and maybe this is a step on Maddie's journey." Holy smokes, he sounded like one of those touchy-feely advice columns that Finn Dawson was addicted to, and had read aloud while they drove to the next performance.

"What doesn't kill you makes you stronger?" Dillon asked.

"Hey. I'm living proof of that." Although he wasn't. He wasn't stronger—not physically, anyway. As to mentally…yeah. He was still floundering there, too. Maybe that saying was all wet.

Dillon suddenly turned and looked over the seat.

"Tow chain there?" Sean had already checked, but Dillon didn't need to know that.

"It is." Dillon settled in his seat, once again facing forward, watching the lazy flakes melt on the windshield. "I'm a sucky tow-ee by the way. Dad says I ride the brakes too much."

"That will be bad in the snow."

"Good thing we brought the old truck," Dillon said.

Sean was beginning to wish they'd brought Maddie along. He had a feeling that she knew how to be towed. Most ranch kids did…except Dillon apparently. He smiled in spite of himself, but it faded quickly, and he hoped Dillon didn't notice.

"I guess I'll be driving this beast until I get a new radiator and grill."

"I could drive you to town."

Dillon shook his head. "Not necessary.

I'll send Dad some photos and explain what happened tonight. Tell him I'm driving the truck now."

Sean wondered if it might be better to simply let Max and Shirl enjoy the first days of their vacation, but decided that Dillon knew what was best as far as his parents were concerned.

Cody had stopped next to Dillon's pickup, which wasn't that far off the road, but was fully impaled on a stub of a branch.

"I thought I'd flag traffic just in case."

Okay. So he was showing signs of being an okay guy. That didn't make what he'd done to Maddie okay, although a small part of Sean thought that he wasn't totally unhappy that they'd broken up.

For Maddie's sake, of course. He was glad that she'd dodged the bullet. That was all. And the fact that he wanted to put an arm around her shoulders, but had settled for pressing his arm against hers as she faced off with her ex…well, that was just a matter of instinct. Of course it was an uncomfortable situation for her, and he wanted her to know she wasn't alone.

Who would expect their ex to show up accidentally on a snowy night?

A few minutes later Sean discovered that while Dillon might be a self-professed bad tow-ee, he knew his way around a tow chain. First, he hooked it to the rear frame beneath the bumper, allowing Sean to pull the truck off the tree, then once it was situated parallel to the road, he switched to the front while Sean put his rig in position to pull the truck back onto the road. Cody flagged him in, and Dillon attached the chain to the GMC's rear hitch. He got into the truck and told Cody he was good to go. Cody waved at Sean, who eased forward. The slack chain went taut, jerking Dillon's truck, and then the little blue beast began to move slowly up onto the road.

He saw Cody making movements with hands, indicating which way Dillon should turn the wheels to straighten them, then less than a minute later, they had the truck on the snowy pavement.

Sean walked back to double-check the chain, then he said to Cody, "I appreciate the help."

"Not a problem." He glanced past Sean in the direction of the Lucky Creek, which Sean took as his cue to drop a warning.

"Steer clear of her for a while."

Cody turned a surprised gaze his way. "Excuse me?"

Sean saw no need to repeat what had been a pretty clear directive.

Cody's eyes narrowed. "You're warning me off?"

"Maddie and I go back a ways. I don't like seeing her upset."

The eyes narrowed even more. "As I understand things, you also upset her."

"She talked about me?" If Sean had taken a moment to reflect, he wouldn't have blurted out the question, but the damage was done.

"We watched the National Finals Rodeo last year. After your ride, Maddie told me she knew you and she told me how."

"Yeah. Well, we all change, don't we. Change our appearances, change our occupations…change our minds."

Cody took the hit fairly well. "None of your business, is it?"

"Nope," Sean said cheerfully. Dillon was

seated behind the wheel of his truck, craning his neck to watch the action, possibly hoping to get to break up a fight. "But I don't want to see Maddie hurting any more than she has to."

Cody started to say something, then stopped. "I have every intention of steering clear. I didn't know she was on the property, or I would have let Dillon out at the gate like he asked. But again, this is between Maddie and me. It's nothing to do with you."

Sean gave a nod, having made his point. It really wasn't his business, but he walked back to his truck feeling better knowing that Cody wouldn't be haranguing Maddie in person on the Lucky Creek Guest Ranch. Because if he did, then Sean had thoughts on the matter.

Dillon actually wasn't too bad of a towee, despite his disclaimer. He almost brought Sean's rig to a stop when he hit the brakes on the corner instead of riding them, but they made it through the gate and onto the ranch, where Sean pulled them parallel to the big barn. He got out of the truck and stopped Dillon, who was about to disconnect the chain.

"Unless you plan on replacing the radiator yourself—" which Sean had no problem with as long as he got to supervise "—we'd better leave the chain on so I can take you to a repair place before school tomorrow."

"I'm going to call Dad and ask him what to do, but I'm sure he's going to want to fix it here."

"Sounds good."

They unhooked the chain and stowed it in the GMC, then started toward the lodge with measured steps, neither in a hurry to get to their respective abodes, despite the sudden dip in temperature.

"I know she says it's no big deal, but I kind of hate coming face-to-face with Maddie after bringing that guy home."

"It won't be a problem." Maddie was inherently kind, and she wouldn't make a teenager feel rotten even if she herself felt rotten.

"He was kind of helpful," Dillon finally said.

"He was," Sean agreed.

They stopped at the point where Sean would head off to his cabin and Dillon to the main lodge.

"He could have told her earlier," Dillon said. "I mean, it's better now than at the church on their wedding day, but all the same…"

"Agreed."

Dillon kicked at the snow, then lifted his gaze, digging his hands more deeply into his pockets as he said, "I guess we'll just have to make sure that she has a good Christmas. And maybe…" he made a face "…plan something to take her mind off her wedding day?"

"I don't know," Sean said slowly. "Maybe that's something she needs to take care of herself."

Dillon smiled. "Yeah. Maybe so. I appreciate the help with the truck."

"Just as we'll appreciate your help with the tree, which we'll tackle tomorrow when you come home from wrestling practice alone—with your vehicle in one piece."

As Sean had hoped, Dillon found the remark darkly amusing. He gave Sean a fake scowl. "I just realized that the GMC isn't licensed. I'll have to drive Mom's car, and there's no way I'm going to come back home if I mess up Sylvia."

Sean frowned and Dillon added, "The car. Sylvia. Mom named it."

"As one does." It sounded exactly like something Shirl would do. "Does it have snow tires?"

"I'm sure it does."

"Maybe we could take a look?"

"Sure. She's parked in the barn in the tractor spot."

Sylvia, a deep blue vintage Volvo station wagon in pristine shape, did indeed have all-weather tires. Sean would have preferred studs for the kid, but the tires were adequate.

"The right front is low," Dillon pointed out. He headed around the back of the car to the air compressor and turned it on. The machine roared to life and then Dillon expertly filled the tire and checked the others. "Good to go," he said before glancing at the dusty clock hanging above the narrow workbench. "And I'll still have time to work on the Giving Tree cards tonight."

"The Giving Tree?"

"My Leadership Club puts it on every year. Kids whose parents have taken some financial hits get presents. We're like really careful in how we go about it, so that nobody feels like they're poor or anything."

"Nice."

"Yeah. Ms. Bartlett is pretty cool about these things. We set it up in the bank next to the café and I'm in charge of the cards that tell whether it's a boy or girl, ages and wish lists and stuff like that."

"I may give it a look after it's set up."

"You should," Dillon said earnestly as they headed toward the barn door.

As they let themselves out, Sean caught sight of Maddie through the window of the lodge moving in the direction of her room with something that looked a lot like a wine bottle in her hand.

Sean hoped that she was able to blow off the encounter with her ex more easily than Dillon had.

Not that you're worried about her...

"I guess I'll call Dad now. See what he wants to do."

"Want me to talk to him?"

Dillon shook his head. "Dad understands these things."

"If you want to tackle the repairs before he gets home, tell him I'll help you."

Dillon grinned. "That'd be great. Thanks."

"Question." Dillon's eyebrows rose, and Sean continued, "Are you ever in a bad mood?" Because he remembered himself being closed off during his teen years. He'd had a good relationship with his parents, but he'd liked to go his own way. Do things his folks might not have approved of. He'd been wild in a lot of ways, while Dillon seemed very…centered.

"Oh, yeah," Dillon replied. "But I've got a lot to be glad about, so…" he shrugged "… I just kind of focus on that."

CHAPTER SEVEN

Got a situation here...

MADDIE FIRED OFF the group text to Whit and Kat, using the code they'd developed in high school to alert one another when life took an interesting, sometimes dramatic turn—but not so dramatic that it warranted a phone call, such as when one was dumped by a fiancé six weeks before the wedding.

The "situation" texts were now few and far between as they'd left the drama of the teen and early college years behind, so when those words appeared on the screen, responses were usually quick—as they were in this case. Only instead of a text, Maddie heard the familiar chimes of a video call coming through.

"Maddie!" Both Whitney and Kat's faces appeared on the screen. Whit's dark blond hair was tucked up under a cowboy hat and Kat had a silk wild rag around her neck fastened with an engraved silver concho.

"Are you together? I mean obviously you are together, but where? Vegas or Reno? I haven't looked at the schedule lately." But she did like to keep track of her friends.

Less than a year ago, Kat had bought her aunt's farm and taken residence, only to be surprised by the arrival of a retired rodeo rider, Troy Mackay, who thought he had a right to the place. Instead he'd been scammed by Kat's cousin, and feeling responsible, she'd offered to let him and his baby daughter, Livia, stay. One thing had led to another, and Troy and Kat fell in love. Troy went back to the rodeo and now he was in the final stretch of his special rodeo tour, The Unrideable. Kat traveled with him when she could to help care for Livia.

Whit's presence on the call was a surprise. The last Maddie knew, her friend had been at home in Missoula.

"We're in Reno," Whit said. "I had a conference in Sacramento, so I popped over to see the action. I'm heading back to Missoula tomorrow."

"What's the situation?" Kat asked.

"Cody," Maddie said simply. "He came by the ranch tonight—"

"What? No!" Whit and Kat chimed in simultaneously.

Maddie explained how Dillon had run off the road and Cody had come to the rescue.

"It wasn't purposeful." Kat sounded skeptical.

"No. But it was… I don't know. *Weird* is the only word I can think of."

"Why weird?" Kat asked with a frown.

"Well, I felt angry for the first time. Like blazing angry."

"Good," Whit said.

"But after the anger died down, I felt… relief." It still kind of boggled her. "Like buckets of relief." Good-riddance relief. "He should have told me his true feelings a long time ago, but he didn't. After an oversize glass of wine," Maddie lifted the nearly empty stemware in a salute, "I realized that I was angrier about him not telling me the truth in a timely manner than I was sad about him leaving. I was supposed to marry him in a matter of weeks. How does that make sense?"

"It's early days," Kat said. "You're probably going to feel a lot of conflicting emotions. You guys were together for what? Three years?"

"A little more. I thought I knew him and then I find out…" Her voice trailed as a thought occurred. "I guess I did know him, because I sensed that something was off, but I didn't—"

"Put the screws on him and force him to confess?" Whit asked.

"I expected my fiancé to be up-front with me without putting the screws on him." Her voice wavered slightly as she said, "I trusted him to tell me the truth."

"Once trust is broken…" Whit said softly.

"It makes it hard to take people at their word," Maddie said. "And I like trusting people. It's—"

"In your nature," Whit finished for her.

It was. She was trusting by nature, but now not so much, even though she wanted to believe that this was a one-off. Her gut had said one thing, her heart another. She'd gone with the heart. Big mistake.

Her friends fell silent, concerned expressions on their faces.

"I wish I could hug you," Kat finally said.

"I would like that very much," Maddie replied.

"I'll be back before Christmas," Kat said. "Hopefully my house is still standing. James is staying there to look after the horses."

Kat's brother was a bit of a bull in a china shop, so Maddie understood the concern, but Kat needed someone to care for the horses she boarded. James might have a disproportionate number of disasters and near misses, but he was excellent with animals.

"I'm sure it'll be fine," Maddie said. "James helped me unload my stuff at your parents' ranch and nothing got dropped."

"Are you sure it was James?" Kat asked.

"Positive," Maddie answered on a laugh. She was starting to feel better, more centered, thanks to her friends. And, yes, a call was better than a flurry of texts. Easier on the thumbs, too.

"I'll travel down from Missoula when Kat gets home from the tour," Whit promised. "We'll have a weekend together."

"I need it," Maddie said. She had a sneaking suspicion that her friends would also be with her on her canceled wedding day, which she truly appreciated.

"How's everything else?" Whit asked.

Maddie spent a few minutes describing her stay at the Lucky Creek, the decorating and upcoming open house before promising to call if any other "situations" popped up. What she did not mention was Sean Arteaga. She'd started to, then stopped. There was no reason not to mention the protective way he'd stood with her in the driveway, facing off with Cody, except that she didn't want to. Not even with her closest friends.

Yet another thing to think about late at night.

Maddie sighed aloud and picked up the wineglass, drained the last drops, then headed to the kitchen to rinse it. The house was dark except for a single light in the kitchen. She walked past the empty spot where the Christmas tree would eventually stand, skirted the train tracks and padded down the short hall to the kitchen. Talking to her friends had helped, more because of the reassurance that she had backup than because of any wisdom imparted. Kat and Whit were on her side, and so, it seemed, were Dillon and Sean.

She turned on the faucet and rinsed the crystal glass then dried it with a microfiber towel before restoring it to the glass-fronted cupboard. The house was warm, quiet and surprisingly cozy feeling for such a large dwelling. She turned and leaned back against the sink, staring at her reflection in the dark windows.

The Maddie Kincaid who'd been slated to marry Cody Marsing was no more; a new woman stood in her place. One who would pay attention to red flags in the future.

DARKNESS STILL PRESSED on the windows when Sean put his feet on the chilly cabin floor. The Lucky Creek Ranch welcomed guests from April until October, so, due to the unpredictable Montana weather during late spring and early fall, the heating system was state-of-the-art, and within seconds of turning on the electric baseboard heaters, the bedroom began to warm.

Sean rubbed a hand over his forehead as he headed for the coffeepot, sidestepping the saddle he'd brought in the day before and had left tipped up onto its fork. He found cleaning and oiling leather therapeutic and since the guy who'd quit at the end of the most recent season hadn't bothered giving the gear a final cleaning, Sean had a lot of therapy ahead of him. He'd finished up four saddles and had ten more to go.

Coffee grounds spilled on the counter as he measured heaping spoons into the brewing basket. He poured the water and turned on the machine, willing it to hurry itself along before scooping the scattered grounds into his hand and dumping them into the sink.

Then he let out the breath he hadn't realized he was holding and leaned back against the counter, crossing his bad leg over his good. Finn had called after Sean returned to his cabin the previous evening and the conversation was still weighing on him. Yes, he'd asked about jobs, and the one Finn was pointing him toward was a good one—if he wanted to manage live-stock and commit to a multiyear contract.

Frankly, he'd love to manage livestock, however, that would put his employment status at the mercy of the owner. He'd known more than one cowboy who'd worked for decades on a ranch, only to have the property sell and then be out of a job in their fifties or sixties, with little retirement to their name.

A story as old as time—at least in the ranching communities, where rich people snapped up ranches as investments or hideaways. Montana was rife with that, and the ranch he was interviewing for was a classic. The current owners of Snow Crest Ranch could make a killing if they chose to sell, potentially leaving him out in the cold.

He needed a profession that allowed him the security he'd happily done without during his rodeo days. The injury coupled with the realization of how fast his savings could and would evaporate, had had a sobering effect on his devil-may-care outlook on life. That said, he would interview for Snow Crest Ranch in the hopes of talking them into a one-year contract. Perhaps, after that year, he'd decide he'd rather manage livestock than go to school, even though that felt a lot like his decision to rodeo rather than go to college—a live-for-now kind of decision that wouldn't serve him well in the future.

You need to bite the bullet and go to school instead of taking the easy-for-now route.

School was expensive, but after he was done, he could write his own ticket, due to the demand for diesel mechanics.

Sean eyed the coffeepot, which was taking its own sweet time, then pushed off the counter and switched the pot with a ceramic cup, allowing the brew to drip directly into the Lucky Creek Ranch mug.

He'd just switched the pot back into place and was about to lift the cup to his lips when a deep rumble from the direction of the barn had him setting the cup back down. He knew that sound and needed to do something about it before it woke everyone on the ranch. And later today, he'd explain to Dillon the importance of switching off the power to the air compressor after he was done airing tires.

THE SUN HAD yet to crest the trees behind the barn when Maddie let herself out of the lodge. Her boots crunched the snow as she headed to the barn, intent on shutting off whatever machine had suddenly come to life in there. Her first thought when she'd heard the engine had been that Sean was warming up a tractor earlier than usual, but a quick glance out the bay windows assured her that the tractors were parked close to the barn and plugged into the engine block heaters. They were definitely not running.

Her second thought was that Sean was using the air compressor—at 6 a.m. Probably not.

Her third thought was that she should investigate instead of pacing the house waiting for the day to start. She'd slept well, but once she'd come awake at 4 a.m., she couldn't go back to sleep. After giving up and making herself a pot of coffee, she'd first sat at the kitchen table sipping and contemplating in the semidarkness, then had adjourned to the main hall where she avoided the temptation of seeing if Santa really fell out of the first car of the train at the end table corner. Instead she'd turned on a single lamp and started unpacking bubble-wrapped angels and Santas, placing the figurines on the enormous coffee table that sat between four leather sofas.

The silence felt comforting, and she focused on bubble wrap and figurines with laser-like intensity because she didn't want to dwell on the fact that her reality for the past several months hadn't been reality at all. She'd been living in a different world than her fiancé.

She didn't know how she felt about Cody. Didn't know if she should be angry or grateful. Being brought back to earth was not an easy thing and she was uncertain how to process not only the change in her life, but the change in her perspective. As she'd realized the night before, she wasn't the same woman Cody had asked to be his wife, and he was not the same man who'd proposed. They'd eased apart during their sixteen-month engagement, and she didn't know how that had happened. It worried her, made her uncertain about future relationships.

Did she even want a future relationship? Lots of people carved out a satisfying life on their own. It was certainly safer. Less worrisome.

Easier.

She pulled in a deep breath as she approached the barn, the cold air stinging the inside of her nostrils, then undid the latch and pushed open the barn door—or tried to. It hit something solid and bounced toward her. Surprised at the rebound, Maddie took a stumbling step backward, catching a heel. Sean emerged from the doorway as she started to fall and took an awkward step forward, holding out a hand, but it was too late for him to stop the forces of gravity. Maddie went over, landing on her butt in the snow.

"Are you okay?"

Maddie ignored the hand he held out as she picked herself up. Once she was on her feet, and had brushed herself off, she gave him a frowning once-over. The man in front of her wore faded jeans jammed into the top of his partially laced work boots, and a flannel shirt buttoned halfway up.

"Where is your coat?" she asked as she took a few swipes at the snow on the seat of her pants.

"I'm a Montanan. Impervious to cold."

"That wasn't the question."

"Dillon left the air compressor on. It lost enough pressure to trigger the automatic start."

"I noticed," she said. "Still didn't answer the question."

He ran his hands over his upper arms, giving lie to "I'm a Montanan impervious to cold" schtick. "I didn't want the compressor to wake you guys up."

The confession touched her because it was, well, thoughtful. "I've been up for a while," she said in a voice that didn't invite follow-up questions. He had the necessary information to piece together why she might have had a restless night.

"Would you like some coffee?"

Maddie gave him a cautious look. "An invitation to the lair?"

"Cabin, Maddie. We started calling them cabins."

She wasn't certain why she didn't want to let go with a grin, but decided to follow her gut, which said, *Be cautious*. It also said, *More coffee sounds good*.

"Sure." This was the first day of the rest of her life, after all. Why not start it by having coffee with a man who confused her? A guy who at this very moment appeared to be looking for signs that she was about to crumble. Maybe her sense that he'd wanted to protect her the night before had been dead-on.

Sean led the way along the path to his cabin, limping more than usual, probably due to the freezing temperatures and early hour. Warm light filtered from beneath the curtain of the front window, giving the cabin a welcoming non-lair look.

They stomped the snow off their boots,

then Sean opened the door and ushered Maddie inside. She stood on the mat just inside the door, warmth from the floor heaters wafting over her as she took in the neat interior of the cabin. Sean was apparently a guy who believed in keeping everything in its place, with the exception of the saddle in the middle of the floor.

"You're cleaning saddles?"

He came out of the kitchen area carrying two mugs and set them on opposite sides of the small oak table. "They need it."

"Next you'll be feeding orphan kittens."

He scowled. "It was only that one time," he said gruffly.

"Don't worry. I won't tell."

His smirk made her smile. She didn't feel like smiling, but there was something about his quasi-grumpy attitude that made a smile necessary. "You're a fraud, Sean Arteaga."

"How so?"

"You're all 'I'll sail my ship alone,' but secretly you're..." she didn't want to say *nurturing* because that wasn't the word "...a caregiver." That, too, was inadequate, but it got her meaning across. She could tell by his affronted expression.

"How so?"

"Kittens for one. The way you are with Dillon for two." She hesitated, then added, "The way you were with me last night. When Cody was here." *When you protected me*.

Protector. That was the word she was looking for, but it was too late to change.

"I just like to do what's right. That's all."

Like reassuringly pressing his arm against hers while she faced off with her ex last night. She'd felt stronger because of it.

She nodded as she contemplated her coffee cup. "There's nothing wrong with that, you know. Caretaking, I mean." And protecting.

She was answered by an upward quirk of his lips that was more of a smirk than a smile. She was not put off. In fact, his dismissive expression only made her want to forge on, but she didn't have a chance to because Sean took advantage of her silence.

"We should get that tree up today."

"Without Dillon?"

"If we have to. It's only nine feet tall."

Maddie thought it was closer to twelve after inspecting it yesterday.

"With a ten-inch trunk." And he'd mentioned being concerned about his leg giving out.

"Eleven. I measured. Max must have had the stand specially made."

"Yay."

He saluted her with his cup, then drank. Unfortunately, the cup hid his mouth, but not his eyes. She'd always found them stunning, gray-blue rimmed in navy with rays of white and specks of gold. And the way his eyes crinkled at the corners kind of did something to her...not that they crinkled all that often because Sean didn't smile all that often.

But sometimes she made him smile, and the effect could be devastating, even when they'd butted heads back in the day.

"I guess if you're going to call me a *caretaker*," he said, lifting his lip in a comical sneer on the last word, "then I'm free to ask how you're doing after last night."

She regarded him for a silent moment.

"Are you evening the score or actually asking?"

His expression sobered. "I'm asking."

She opened her mouth, pulled in a breath, then closed it again. "It's complicated."

He didn't ask how, and Maddie offered nothing else. She drank her coffee to the halfway mark, then set the cup down and pushed back her chair. "I should go. I'd planned to feed the horses after turning off the engine." Instead she'd been knocked on her butt in the snow and then lured to a lair with the promise of coffee.

Sean also pushed back his chair. "I'll come with you. Maybe you can open gates for me when I feed the cattle."

"Of course." She'd wanted to help with the feeding chores all along, but someone stubbornly refused.

"Just…give me a sec." He headed to one of the two doors at the far end of the room and disappeared into the bedroom, where she heard him digging around in what sounded like a duffel bag. A few minutes later he emerged from the room wearing wool socks and buttoning a flannel shirt over a waffle weave Henley.

"Good to go."

As Maddie got to her feet, she let out a silent breath. The man was something. Tall and lean with broad shoulders; solid muscle, as a bronc rider should be. But it wasn't his physique that drew her attention—although it had that power—but rather the layers that she was uncovering. The puzzle that was Sean Arteaga. Cranky horseman. Defender of orphan kittens and jilted fiancées. Things she was still wrapping her mind around as he closed the cabin door behind them, and they headed to the barn to feed first the horses and then the cattle.

She yawned as she walked, a wave of exhaustion hitting her despite the recent intake of caffeine. Maybe she hadn't slept as well as she'd thought. Or maybe reaction was setting in. As she'd told Sean, her feelings about Cody were complicated, as was her rather startling realization that the woman she'd become over the past two weeks would never consider becoming Mrs. Cody Marsing, even if he came crawling back.

But that didn't mean she didn't hurt. And it didn't mean that the simmering anger she felt toward the man who'd dumped her was gone. She was human, after all.

It was hard on the brain, and, frankly, she was looking forward to some mindless Christmas prep and the certainty that she wouldn't have to deal with Cody again.

But if she did, she knew that Kat, Whit, Dillon *and* Sean had her back. She wasn't alone.

CHAPTER EIGHT

CARETAKER. RIGHT.

A caretaker wouldn't have put his rodeo career ahead of personal relationships, as Sean had done not once, but twice in his life, but he wasn't going to make the mistake of trying to get Maddie to understand that.

They parted company at the tractors, Maddie continuing to the barn to throw hay for the horses in the rear corral, while he unplugged the engine block heater and started the tractor.

Before Maddie disappeared into the barn, Dillon hailed them and jogged through the deep snow, oblivious to the fact that he was wearing sneakers.

"Just wanted to let you guys know that I'm slated for a late practice, so if I don't get home on time, that's why."

"Maybe you could shoot a text to one of

us before you leave town?" Maddie suggested.

"Sure thing." He turned to Sean, who'd joined Maddie at the barn door. "I talked to the garage guy. He's ordering the radiator, but he's booked solid and can't put it in."

"Then we'll do it."

"Excellent." Dillon grinned. "I asked Dad and like I thought, he's good with it."

"Great. We'll start as soon as the parts come in."

"And in the meantime, I'll try not to wrap Sylvia around any trees." He cleared his throat. "I'll come home alone, too."

"No worries," Maddie said. "In fact, I'm glad it happened. Now when I run into him in Larkspur, and I will, it'll be easier."

Dillon's entire body seemed to relax on her lightly spoken words. "One more thing." Maddie tilted her head and Sean simply waited, wondering at the kid's wary tone. "I think we should put the tree up before I go to school, since I won't be home in time to help."

"Won't you be late if we do?"

Dillon cleared his throat. "I already cleared

it with the attendance office. Told them I'm having car troubles. I just need a verification note..."

Maddie and Sean exchanged looks, then Maddie shrugged. "Why not?"

So it was that they wrestled and wrangled a tree that was definitely taller than nine feet through the double doors and into the main hall, situating it on its side next to the windows where it would be visible to anyone outside—visitors to the open house, the photographer for the newspaper and any delivery folk who stopped by in their big brown trucks. Not that many people after the open house was over.

"You guys do all of this simply for the community open house?" Sean said as he caught his breath. His leg was protesting the weight he'd tried not to put on it, but he'd ended up closest to the end, his face smashed against branches that were still bound to the trunk with twine.

"Pretty much," Dillon replied. "And for the family before we go south. There's a community competition and Mom's won almost every year. It's good public relations and that's what Lucky Creek Guest Ranch is all about."

Sean's lips twitched at the kid's spiel. Dillon winked. "I should do commercials, right?"

"Definitely," Maddie said. She wiped her hands down the sides of her pants. "Ready?"

"As I ever will be," Sean replied.

Getting the tree upright, then lifting it enough to get the oversize trunk into the oversize tree stand was just as difficult and awkward as Sean had thought it would be, even with a wrestler doing the brunt of the work.

"The problem," Dillon said after they'd finally gotten the tree into the base, "is that there's no good way to hang on. I suggested a block and tackle system after I took physics, but Mom won't let me mess with the ceiling."

Sean laughed and started to lower himself to the ground to tighten the screws in the holder, but Maddie said, "I'll do that. You guys need to get this monster straight."

Which, it turned out, took longer than dragging the tree in and setting it up. But finally, Dillon was satisfied with the angle, the stand was secured, and Maddie got up on the floor, brushing stray needles off her sweater.

"Do you want us to put the lights on while you're gone?" she asked.

"And anything else that you might want to," Dillon replied. "There are photos in the album, but as far I'm concerned, you can do what you want. We still have a ton of stuff to do outside this weekend. Also, Mom texted me that the reindeer should arrive any day now."

"Reindeer?" Sean said.

"Special order. They go with the sleigh we park near the gate. Mom's been looking for the perfect deer for a long time and found them on Etsy this fall. Custom-made out of bent branches or something."

"Cool," Maddie said, wondering what a bent-branch reindeer looked like. She glanced at the clock, then said, "I'll write that note."

They left the house together, Dillon and Maddie heading to the barn where Sylvia the Volvo was parked, and Sean to the tractor.

"I'll see you tonight," Dillon called to him. "Don't get tinsel poisoning or anything."

"We'll do our best to avoid it," Sean assured him solemnly before climbing into the tractor cab. His leg was not happy with the extra stress he'd inadvertently put on it while wrestling the tree, but he figured that after feeding the cattle he'd spend the rest of the day on light duty. How hard could it be putting lights on a tree?

The engine and the hydraulics had just come up to temperature when Maddie came around the corner of the barn. Sean leaned across the cab to push open the door, as tractor etiquette required, but she didn't climb the steps.

"I'll walk to the first gate." Which led to an empty corral he had to pass through on the way to the field. The cattle were hugged up against the second gate, which had usually caused him trouble, and he'd finally settled on letting them wander out as he drove the tractor in, because they inevitably turned around and followed the food.

Instead of getting into the tractor after opening the first gate, Maddie waved him through, then walked ahead of him to the second. After shooing the cows away and opening it at the very last minute to let the tractor through, she then closed it and walked to the cab, rubbing her hands over the arms of her coat. It was cold outside, and Sean popped open the door as she climbed the steps. A second later she settled in the jump seat and suddenly the cab smelled really good. Like flowers. And a little spice. Feeding normally smelled like alfalfa, which he was allergic to, so he decided to embrace the change.

They were rolling across the field to the haystack when Sean's phone rang. He pulled off his glove with his teeth, checked the screen and answered, recognizing the number of the McCullough Diesel Mechanics Institute.

"This is Sean Arteaga."

"Good morning, Mr. Arteaga. This is Larry Skerrit with MDMI." A brief pause, then, "You've got some serious background noise there."

Sean slowed the tractor to a stop, dropping the engine to a still-loud idle while avoiding Maddie's curious gaze.

"I'm in the middle of morning chores," he explained. "I'm glad you called."

"I have some news about admissions, probably best discussed when you aren't in the middle of chores." Sean's stomach tightened at the ominous words, and he was about to say that he could talk, when Mr. Skerrit said, "Would you be available at say, eleven o'clock, if I were to call again?"

If Maddie hadn't been next to him, he would have shut the tractor down and talked then and there, because he wanted to know why the man had called. Was he no longer wait-listed? Had someone bumped him from his position? He was far enough down on the list that he knew he wasn't getting in this year, so…

But Maddie *was* there, so he said, "Sure. That sounds good. I'll wait for your call."

"Speak to you soon."

Sean pocketed the phone and put the tractor back into gear. Without looking at Maddie, he said, "I'm considering some educational options." Fancy talk for a one-year training program, that he was now half-afraid he wasn't going to get into. Maybe his high school grades had been taken into consideration? He hadn't been the greatest student, but it wasn't because he didn't understand the material. It was more a matter of where his priorities had lain.

"You're looking at going back to school?"

"Why the surprise?" Her surprise wasn't exactly insulting, but it nudged up against it.

"I guess because... I don't know. Preconceived notions maybe?"

"Always dangerous," he said as they approached the haystack, outpacing the cows that had been milling around the tractor when he'd stopped. "Best hurry," he said when Maddie hesitated with her hand on the door handle.

"Yes," she agreed, shooting a quick look at the approaching cattle. "Then I can get back inside and ask you a couple hundred questions."

And with that small threat, she was gone.

MADDIE DID HAVE QUESTIONS, but to her credit, on the drive back to the barn she did not ask even one—maybe because Sean was fiercely directing his attention toward the track in front of the tractor. One would have thought he was driving a curvy mountain road instead of heading through a field with no obstacles in sight.

Sean shut off the tractor and followed Maddie down the steps, grimacing as his injured leg contacted solid earth. He closed the tractor door, then said, "Diesel mechanic school."

"Congratulations."

"Thank you."

He spoke in a way that made her want to ask if he was nervous, but she smiled instead A split second later he answered her smile.

A sense of tenuous camaraderie warmed her even as her logical side took control. They were two people at turning points in their lives. It would be easy to confuse mutual needs and similar life circumstances with camaraderie. She wasn't going to make that mistake. She had enough on her mind wondering why she hadn't realized that Cody was falling out of love long ago... and that she might have been, too.

WHILE SEAN WAITED for eleven o'clock to roll around, he finished oiling the saddle on his living room floor. This was not good, this call that he was waiting for. Thankfully, Finn had lined up the interview with Snow Crest Ranch two days after Christmas, so he had a backup plan, and it felt like he was going to need it.

The phone rang at eleven sharp, and Sean realized he felt very much like he had when he'd been on deck at a rodeo. Adrenaline surged at the ring, and then the calm followed as he accepted the call.

"This is Sean Arteaga."

"Larry Skerrit. MDMI. How are you doing today?" Without waiting for a reply, the man plunged on. "Thank you for taking my call. I have a situation here."

The knot in Sean's stomach tightened as he prepared himself to hear that the school was closing. They were kicking him off the wait list. Whatever. Instead, Mr. Skerrit said, "I have a note here that you won't be filing for financial aid."

"I saved enough to where I don't need it." He wasn't going to become part of the student loan nightmare if he could help it. If he couldn't pay, he wasn't going to school.

"Well…we have an unexpected opening and neither of the people above you on the wait list are prepared to take the position due to financials. In order to be accepted, we need the full tuition payment December 29. Classes start January 15."

"I could do that," Sean said slowly. He moistened his lips. "I'd kind of been expecting bad news."

"If you're able to attend, I'd say this is good news."

"I'm in the perfect position, Mr. Skerrit." Nothing tying him down, and Maddie was fully capable of feeding the cattle, as she'd intended to when she'd first arranged to stay at the guest ranch. He hated leaving it to her, but he couldn't let this opportunity slip away. "Shall I mail the tuition—"

"We'll send information for you to pay online."

"Of course."

Mr. Skerrit outlined the procedure, told him to watch his inbox.

"So I transfer the money by December 29, and I'm good to go?"

"You are. Welcome aboard. You'll be receiving quite a few emails with information shortly, including links to temporary housing. We don't have actual housing options, but keep a resource list of landlords who rent almost exclusively to our students."

"Sounds good."

"Very well, then. If you have any questions, please do not hesitate to contact the main office and they'll connect you to the answer."

"Thanks. I appreciate the call."

Sean let out a breath and leaned back in his chair, feeling ridiculously drained. He'd expected to get the boot and instead he got accepted.

Everything worked out.

Sean gave a mental eye roll.

It worked out except for Maddie, who would deal with the brunt of the ranch work once he started school. Maybe he could hire someone to help, because he hated leaving her to deal alone, even with the help of Dillon, the teen wonder.

MADDIE PUT THE finishing touches on her bridal dress sketches, having transferred them to heavy paper and then made notes of the specifics. Silk chiffon for the Ginger Rogers designs, tulle and satin for the punk cowgirl. The designs were too large to scan properly but she'd photographed them, emailing copies to Danna and Ashley along with the promise to leave the originals at Spurs and Veils for further consideration. The nice thing was that she had been able to complete sketches that she was proud of, which meant she was probably not too far from being able to deal with happy brides again.

Did she *want* to deal with happy brides?

Or did she want to hang on to this jaded feeling, which had her looking at matters with a different perspective? Frankly, the jaded feeling wasn't that bad.

As ten o'clock rolled around, she put the sketches in a tube carrier, then jumped as the doorbell rang. Obviously it wasn't Sean, who rapped on the doorframe as he entered the lodge.

When she got to the door, the brown truck

was driving away, leaving behind four very large cardboard boxes. The special order reindeer, no doubt—the last of the decorating. She and Sean and Dillon had spent the weekend stringing lights and arranging outdoor decorations and now it appeared that the end was in sight.

Maddie pulled on the wool socks she'd taken off while drawing, then put on the boots and jacket she'd left near the back door. By the time she'd let herself out of the house, Sean was headed toward the lodge, hands in his pockets, head down against the lightly swirling snow.

They met at the boxes, and he lifted his gaze to the sky.

"It's just a flurry," Maddie said. "I checked the radar."

Indeed, almost as soon as she spoke, the snow slowed. A moment later the sun came out and Sean dusted off the box closest to him before pulling out his knife to cut the tape on the oversize container. With Maddie's help, he eased the four-foot-tall reindeer out of its box and began unwrapping the padding and bubble wrap.

Once the reindeer was stripped of its protective coverings, Sean gave an approving nod. Indeed, the animal was handsome, crafted out of branches and wearing a collar of evergreen.

"It's going to look really good with the sleigh," Maddie murmured.

They quickly unboxed the second deer, which had its head down, as if grazing. The third, they soon discovered, had parted company with its head. Maddie could see that the head and body had been crafted separately and the branches where the connecting wires had been attached had pulled free.

"Oh, no," Maddie said before taking her phone out of her pocket to snap a few photos so that Shirl would get a refund due to damage.

"I'm glad Dillon is gone," Sean said. "The kid would have a heart attack."

Protector.

"This would be nice for Halloween," Maddie said, glancing up at him. "A little fake blood..."

"How important are the reindeer to the overall scheme of things?"

Maddie inspected the broken head. "We can fix this. Some wire, some more fake evergreens, hot glue…should be a snap." Her mouth tightened on one side. "Well, not necessarily a snap, but it should be doable.

"Do you have what we need?"

"Have you seen Max's shop?" Maddie asked. "If it's not there, I'll eat my hat."

Sean gave her a frowning look.

"What?" she asked.

"My grandmother used to say that."

"So? I'm old at heart."

He made a scoffing sound, then turned his attention to the last box, opening it and pulling out a perfect reindeer. "We could go with three."

"We'll fix this one."

"You're the boss. Max put you in charge. Remember?"

"Mmm."

Sean Arteaga was playing, and she wasn't going to ruin things by making him aware. He might be doing it on purpose, but she suspected that he wasn't…or so she thought until she turned and saw him studying her in a thoughtful way.

"Is something wrong?"

"No."

"Then why are you looking at me like you're trying to come up with a tactful way to tell me I have spinach in my teeth?"

"I guess because I didn't expect you to catch me staring," he said easily, but there were spots of color forming over his cheekbones.

"Do I have spinach in my teeth?" She put her fingers to her lips.

"Your teeth are fine."

"What happened with your phone call?"

He gave a short laugh at the lightning change of topic. "I got into school a year early."

"You did? When do you leave?"

"Middle of January. I'll have to work something out so that I don't leave you with a mess of work in the middle of winter."

Maddie ignored the sinking sensation in her midsection. "Don't worry about me. I'm more than capable of feeding before I go to work. The shop doesn't open until ten o'clock."

There was a roughness to her voice that surprised her. But she didn't want anyone worrying about her. She could take care of herself. She'd been sweet Maddie for so long that she had the sneaking suspicion people underestimated her abilities. Sean seemed to.

When she looked up again, ready to mention that small fact, Sean took her face in his hands, tilting it so that she looked into his eyes. And then, shortly after the jolt that always came when their gazes connected, he lowered his mouth to hers.

Maddie's body went still, her mind went still, then both came awake, and she leaned into him, putting her hands over his, allowing the kiss to deepen until her knees went weak, then somehow, she found the strength to step back.

"What was that?" she asked, her gaze locked on his. He looked as stunned as she was.

"A surprise?" There wasn't a hint of humor in his voice.

"Yes." She picked up the reindeer head from the top of the box next to her and held it between them.

"Maddie, I..."

"Kissed me." It was a bemused observation rather than an accusation.

"Yeah." He ran a hand over his neck. "I did that."

She gave her head a shake as if to clear it. "Well," she said. "I can scratch 'kiss Sean Arteaga' off my bucket list." She lifted the reindeer head a little higher, not because she was afraid of him repeating himself, but because she wasn't comfortable with her response. Kissing Sean Arteaga hadn't been on her bucket list, but it should have been. Hokey smokes.

"I apologize, Maddie."

"You don't need to." If one kiss from another man had this kind of an impact on her, then it was a good thing she wasn't getting married in a few weeks.

She studied him for a moment, then held out the reindeer head. Sean automatically took it, and when he did, she stepped closer, nudging the head aside with her hip and slid her palms up along the bristly planes of his cheeks, taking note of the raised scar where no hair grew. His gaze was both startled and serious as she rose up on her toes and kissed him. Not a sensual kiss like the one he'd given her, because she was afraid of where that might lead. Instead it was a soft meeting of the lips, but even that fleeting contact made her senses whirl.

"There," she said softly, holding out her hands for the reindeer head again. "Now we're even."

Sean cleared his throat. "I guess we are."

Maddie gestured toward the lodge with the head, tapping into her businesswoman persona to say briskly, "I'll get to work on this if you want to see about clearing up the cardboard."

"You're the..." Sean's voice trailed as she gave him the death ray, then he smiled as they eased back to solid ground. They'd kissed. It had been surprising and freeing.

Empowering.

Maddie cocked her head. "This changes things." How could it not?

"It doesn't have to," Sean replied matter-of-factly.

Her eyebrows came together, but she didn't ask the question teetering on her lips, perhaps because she wasn't ready for the answer. Instead she said, "I'd like it if it didn't." She cleared her throat. "Maybe you could be less cranky, but other than that."

He smiled down at her, making her stomach do a tiny free fall, then gently settled his hands on her shoulders and planted a kiss on her forehead.

"So things won't be awkward," he said as he dropped his hands.

Maddie brought her hands together in front of her, no longer having access to the reindeer head. "Now we're no longer even."

"Maybe you can do something about that sometime."

She gave a small sniff. "I never was one for one-upmanship."

Sean grinned again and Maddie indicated the reindeer head. "I should get going on reindeer repairs."

"I'll clean up the cardboard."

By the time Dillon came home, early due to the fact that he was leaving at the crack of dawn the next morning for one of the two pre-holiday wrestling matches, Maddie and Sean were doing what she liked to call "okay." Actually they were doing better than okay, working in harmony, despite her brain tying itself in knots trying to figure out why she wasn't ducking for cover.

Because those were rebound kisses, her little voice finally whispered. *You just got booted from a three-year relationship. You're getting back out there.*

Isn't it a bit soon?

When was too soon? Who was to say?

There was nothing wrong with rebound kisses. Recovery kisses. "Get back in the saddle" kisses. They didn't have to signal a commitment. They were fun. Hot. Distracting.

Were they fair to Sean?

She'd ask, because wondering and worrying got her nowhere. She would be upfront. Make certain that she and the man who was outside with Dillon arranging a garland harness between the sleigh and the surviving reindeer were on the same page.

The page that would turn in short order when he went his way, and she went hers.

"Are you coming?" Dillon opened the door and called into the house.

"On my way."

Maddie carefully carted the reindeer out the front door and Dillon took it from her, carrying it down to its buddies near the sleigh. Once the garland harness was in place, and Maddie and Sean were standing side by side on the porch, Dillon flipped the switch cleverly built into the lodge wall, turning on the power to the outside decorations, and suddenly the hours they'd spent that weekend wrapping newel posts and arranging lights in trees so that there weren't too many blues or reds in one area seemed worthwhile.

"And…*voilà*!" Dillon said.

"Look at his face," Sean said in an undertone while keeping his gaze directed forward at the light display. "For a kid who tried to cancel Christmas, he sure seems happy."

"Yes. I think his cool teenage self was battling his kid self."

"My kid self is happy."

"Is it?"

"I got the train fixed."

Maddie gave him a gentle elbow and he nudged her back as they stood side by side, gazes fixed on the light show in front of them.

It's going to be okay, she thought. *You have a recovery buddy. He understands, and so do you.*

Dillon clambered up the flagstone steps and came to stand beside Sean, pulling in a satisfied breath. "It's plenty dark."

The photographer was due to arrive at six the next day and Dillon had been concerned about it being dark enough to show off the lights. He checked his watch, then said, "Okay. I'll just make the team meeting." Which was at seven o'clock at the coach's home. Instead of practice the night before the match, they were having a team-building event and then Dillon would spend the night at a teammate's house.

"By the way," he said to Sean. "I asked my counselor about MIDM. He said it's a top-notch program. Way to go." He seemed as happy as Sean that things had worked out there.

"And don't even speak of finding a replacement," Maddie added. While they'd been putting finishing touches to the lighted trees outside, Sean had explained how he hoped to talk one of the Farley brothers into helping out until Max came home, but neither Maddie nor Dillon would hear of it.

"We can handle it," Dillon said.

"I can drive a tractor as well as you. I can unfreeze a waterer."

"And remember that we found the fences in stupidly good shape," Dillon added. "Which makes your presence..." he looked skyward as if trying to come up with a word "...superfluous."

"Thanks," Sean said dryly.

Dillon grinned. "Vocab word. Actually you are a *crucial* part of the squad." He lifted his eyebrows in a way that indicated he'd just successfully used another vocab word.

"So glad," Sean muttered, but she could tell that he understood that Maddie and Dillon could handle the guest ranch. There were neighbors they could call if there were issues. Calving started in March, so really, other than maintenance, he wasn't needed. His presence made things easier, but as Maddie pointed out she and Dillon would have been handling the place alone if Max hadn't contacted Sean.

What would that have looked like?

Would she have come to similar conclusions about the changes in her life if Scan hadn't been there? Kisses aside, there was something about his presence that helped her take a long hard look at things she should have looked at earlier. She couldn't say why, but his presence made her *want* to look at those things in a critical light. It made her want to approach life more in the way he did. Pragmatically.

And, if he hadn't been there, she'd never have known how excellently the man could kiss, and while she may never kiss him again, never knowing would have been a loss.

CHAPTER NINE

SEAN WAS GLAD he wouldn't be paying the Lucky Creek Ranch electrical bill. The lights and decorations were tasteful—Shirl would have settled for nothing less—and spread over a wide area, so the lodge didn't look like one of those residential Christmas light shows one saw on YouTube. But there was a lot of twinkling going on.

He found that he didn't mind the twinkling. It reminded him of the camaraderie he shared with Dillon and Maddie, his fellow castaways. He smiled at the thought, but that was what the situation felt like with the three of them living in isolation, even though Dillon came and went. Maybe *he* needed some time on the outside to get his head together.

Or maybe it was just fine as it was.

Kissing Maddie had been…thought-provoking.

He'd leave it at that.

Chicken.

He brushed aside the thought knowing he'd do some deep thinking later, when he had better perspective. Something had shifted after the kiss. Maddie hadn't retreated, which had been his first fear when his lips had reluctantly left hers. He hadn't wanted her to back off, or to feel awkward, if for no other reason than that Dillon would certainly pick up on anything amiss between them. But instead of backing off, she'd accepted his kiss, and evened the score with one of her own. He thought he might have seen her swaggering at one point that evening, but that might have been his imagination.

She understands.

They were in similar circumstances. She wasn't reading anything into the kiss; in fact, he was probably doing more of that than she was.

Because you are on the edge of falling for her.

Sean hit the brakes. That's what came from looking at things too closely. Unwelcome information.

He wasn't going to fall for anyone. Wasn't going to set himself up to be a three-time loser. Rodeo was no longer an issue, but what if it hadn't really been his career that had spoiled his last two relationships? What if it was just him? Maybe there was something about him, his inability to fully engage, that ruined things?

The past is the past. Let it go.

But losing twice had stung, just like losing his rodeo career had stung.

He opened the door to the lodge, and the scent of evergreen and cinnamon met his nostrils. Homey holiday scents. Scents he hadn't experienced in too long, having spent most of his holidays since losing his parents on the road. Maddie sat on the sofa with her feet curled under her. She smiled at him, as if they were still simply ranch mates—which was what he wanted, of course—and invited him over with a gesture of her head.

He felt that now familiar sense of warmth that she seemed to arouse more often than not. Not because he was falling for her, but because she made him feel accepted, bum leg, ugly face and all.

"ALL'S WELL?" Maddie asked as Sean ambled into the main hall and stood a few feet from the sofa where she'd sat while admiring the Christmas tree.

"It's a winter wonderland."

She smiled at the wry words, and while he didn't smile back, his gaze was softer than usual as it rested on her. Friends.

They were friends. She liked the feel of it.

He glanced toward the kitchen, then at the small wet bar. Maddie was about to suggest a libation to take the edge off while they waited for the photographer, but lights cut through the window before she could speak. She craned her neck to see past the tree, and sure enough a vehicle had just executed a sweeping turn and was now coming to a stop on the opposite side of the driveway.

"Surely she's not early?" Maddie said, getting to her feet.

"One way to find out." Sean crossed to the door and swung it open. Maddie joined him at the door as they watched a woman with high cheekbones and sleek chin-length dark hair escaping from under a stocking cap cross the flagstones, a camera bag in one hand and a tripod case in the other.

"Hello," she said as she stepped inside the lodge. The smile she flashed at Sean froze as her gaze landed on the scarred side of his face.

"Sean Arteaga?"

He gave her a curious look, obviously trying to place her. "I'm sorry…"

"No." She gave a short laugh. "You don't know me. I take rodeo photos as a hobby, and I've watched you ride." She frowned at the scar. "I didn't see that ride, however."

Sean gave a tight smile in response, then eased back a step. Maddie wondered if he was even aware that he'd moved.

"Hi," the woman said to Maddie, holding out a hand but offering no introduction. Instead she did a slow circle, taking in the holiday decor. "Wow. This is nice." She flashed another smile at Sean, only this one didn't freeze. "I called to tell you I was running early, but no one answered."

Maddie wondered about that because she'd been in the lodge all afternoon, but maybe the woman had dialed the wrong number.

"I'm Maddie," she said.

"Gwen Tolliver."

"Are you new to the area?" Because Maddie was very involved with the community, and she'd never seen this woman before.

"I am. I got tired of the rat race and decided to follow my passion." Maddie tilted her head politely, and Gwen added, "Photography. I work for the paper to pay the rent, thus allowing me to do my art on the side. Plus, I can write almost everything off my taxes now."

"Smart," Maddie said softly.

"Shall we get started?" Gwen asked. She turned to Sean. "Do you have a Christmas sweater?"

Maddie didn't know which was funnier—the thought of Sean owning a Christmas sweater, or the look of horror on his face.

"No." He cleared his throat. "We were told that we wouldn't be part of the session."

Gwen smiled the confident smile of a person used to getting their way. "Photos have more meaning when people are in them."

"I understood that this was advertising for the open houses," Maddie said. "Shots of the pretty decorations?"

Gwen's focus was on Sean. She openly studied his face, her gaze was more clinical than rude, but Maddie found that she didn't like it one bit, and seeing Sean shift uncomfortably, she liked it even less.

"No one wants to see a scarred guy in a Christmas sweater," Sean said.

"The scar gives you character, especially with your bone structure. And the juxtaposition with a Christmas sweater—"

"No." Maddie was surprised to hear the word leave her mouth. For that matter, everyone seemed surprised at her snap refusal. "I've looked at the shots from previous years and there are no people in them." Maddie forced a smile. "Let's continue the tradition?"

"You're not taking my photo tonight." Sean's voice held a steely undernote.

Gwen looked disappointed, but not abashed. "Okay. I see what you're saying, but would it be possible to arrange a time to take some candid shots? You know, the rodeo hero after retirement. The aftermath of the big ride. People eat that stuff up, and with your bone structure..."

The words petered out as she realized the crowd wasn't buying.

"It would make a great feature," she said stubbornly.

"I don't want to be part of a feature."

"People love this stuff," Gwen repeated, but she bent over and unzipped her camera bag, signaling her reluctant acceptance of his refusal to pose. She pulled out the camera and adjusted some settings. We'll start in here and then move outside when it gets a little darker."

A little over an hour later she was gone.

"Do you think we got the photos that Dillon is hoping for?" Sean asked as the sound of Gwen's car engine caused Maddie's muscles to give a little. She hadn't realized how tense the woman had made her. And what was with the protectiveness toward Sean, who was well able to fight his own battles?

It was totally because of the vulnerable look she'd caught when Gwen had started talking about candid shots and bone structure; a look that had evaporated so quickly that she might have imagined it—but she hadn't. *That* was what had cued her instant protective response.

She would have reacted the same no matter who had been on the receiving end of that tone-deaf request. If Gwen the photographer couldn't see how uncomfortable she'd made—

Maddie brought her thoughts to an abrupt halt and said, "I don't know, but I don't want her back."

Sean rubbed his palm over the injured face, then abruptly dropped his hand, as if not wanting to draw Maddie's eye to the healing scar.

"I don't know," he said in a tone that straddled dark and light. "With my bone structure, a messed-up face and a Christmas sweater, perhaps she could have created great art."

"No doubt," Maddie said dryly. She crossed the room to the main switch bank and started turning off outlets one by one. The room seemed overly dim with only the lamps lighting it, but she didn't mind. She'd had enough twinkling brightness for one day.

Sean pushed his hands into his back pockets. "Like I told you before, I don't like being stared at and the scar just...you know...gives people a reason. One that I can't fault them for because, hey, something out of the ordinary."

People, mainly women, had stared at him before the scar. Maddie knew because she'd worked with him and had watched the guests studying him when he was unaware.

"Who likes to be stared at?" Maddie asked. "Gwen?"

She laughed. The woman had posed the entire time she was shooting her photos, tossing head, making her hair swing to and fro while making artistic gestures. Maddie took her seat on the sofa again, curling her feet under her and leaning on the arm.

"Would you like a drink?" Sean asked. "Max gave us full use of his bar and I don't think we've taken advantage."

"A little one," she said. "Bourbon." Sean nodded and crossed to the far wall where an antique bar salvaged from an old hotel stood ready for service. His limp was slightly more pronounced, but that was probably because he'd made such an effort not to limp while boundary-defiant Gwen had been there.

"I know the feeling about not wanting to get stared at," she said when he handed her two fingers of bourbon in a crystal glass. "Am I not hiding out here with you? Escaping the sympathetic looks of the townsfolk?"

"Yeah. I guess you are."

To her surprise he joined her on the sofa, sitting a couple feet away with his drink held in a hand propped on his thigh.

"I might be done hiding," she said. "Not that I'm over what happened. That's gonna take some time. But..." she lifted the drink to her lips, enjoying the warmth of the golden liquid as it moved over her tongue "... I don't think it's so much losing the guy I thought I loved. It's losing trust."

"Do you love him?"

Had anyone told her a few weeks ago that Sean Arteaga would ask that question of her, she would have scoffed. Now she simply looked at her drink and said, "I love the man I got engaged to. My question is, did he exist?"

"Maybe he changed. People do."

She brought her gaze up to his. "And isn't that scary? How do you know who will change and who won't?"

"Have your other friendships changed?"

Maddie adjusted herself on the sofa, staring at the dark window, no longer lit by the outside lights. "My best friends, no. And Kayla, my business partner, she's been a rock. I really appreciate the way she's given me what I would have had trouble giving myself—a break from the business."

Kayla *had* been great. Elsa, too. Swooping in to protect her, arranging matters so that she didn't have to deal with brides until she felt stronger.

"Do you want to go back?" Sean asked. "To your business?"

She considered for a moment, then said, "It won't be with the same attitude. That's for sure. I'll probably be asking myself 'Will it last?' more often than I ever did before."

"Understandable."

Silence fell, but it wasn't uncomfortable, and Maddie appreciated the fact that despite everything, they could enjoy a quiet moment. She let out a soft breath, then she and Sean turned their heads at the exact same moment, and their gazes connected.

There was no mistaking what he was thinking.

"Are you going to kiss me again?" Maddie asked.

"You're the person who's one behind in the count."

She inched closer, still holding her drink. "But do I want to even the score?"

"Only you can answer that."

She pulled in a breath, smiling a little. "I think I do." She brought her hand to the side of his face, felt his muscles tighten as she lightly touched the raised scar, then relax again she leaned in to kiss him. The contact wasn't as startling as the first time. No, it was warm and welcoming and…she didn't want to say *right*, but it was right.

He smiled into her eyes as she leaned back and then raised her drink to sip.

"You're good for me, Maddie Sunshine."

"I guess I can say the same," she replied softly. "Because you understand."

He raised his drink. "Here's to understanding."

CHAPTER TEN

MADDIE'S SHOULDERS TIGHTENED as automatic chimes played the first few bars of the wedding march when she walked through the front door of Spurs and Veils, carrying the cardboard tube with Danna's dress designs in one hand.

That she did not need. She decided she'd exit through the back.

Elsa poked her head out of the back room and her friendly smile faltered before she gushed, "Maddie!"

She pushed back a few strands of sleek reddish-brown hair as she stepped out of the hallway leading to the fitting area. She was shorter than Maddie, but carried herself in a way that made her seem taller.

"I didn't expect to see you here. I hope you're enjoying your time off."

The color in Elsa's cheeks rose after she spoke, and Maddie felt a wave of empathy.

What does one say to a jilted bride? Especially a jilted bride in a bridal shop.

"I wanted to talk to Kayla about borrowing a dress. Is she back there?"

"Yes." Elsa made an awkward hand movement before asking, "Do you want me to get her?"

"No need. I'll find her."

"Uh…okay." Elsa spoke a little louder than necessary and as Maddie moved past her into the viewing area, Kayla, looking as perfect as ever with her shoulder length blond hair just brushing the shoulders of her off white sweater dress, came out of the "vault" where they stored their new arrivals along with various seasonal items.

"Maddie!" Kayla embraced her, then stepped back. "Are you doing okay?"

"Better than one might expect." She didn't want to discuss herself, so she dived into her reason for coming. "I'm going to leave these for Danna, but she thinks she knows which design she wants to go with. I was thinking that I could use that Bella Mondo sample from two years ago as the base for the dress, but I want to show Ashley and get her thoughts."

She started toward the vault, but Kayla smoothly stepped in front of her. "Why don't you let me drop off the dress."

"Why?"

"I took that dress home a while ago."

Maddie blinked at her, and Kayla sucked a breath in from between her teeth. "I wanted to see how it was constructed, with that inner corset and all, so I…took it home. I'll drop it by Ashley's tomorrow, and you can confer with her then?"

"I…sure." Something was off, but before she could pinpoint it, Kayla put a hand on Maddie's shoulder, turning her and then walking with her to the main part of the store.

They'd barely gotten into the room when something clattered to the floor behind them. Maddie turned, and then Elsa swallowed and said, "Blinken."

"What?"

"My cat is going to the vet. She got loose and is hiding in the back room under the dresses. We…didn't want you to know that we'd lost a cat in the place."

Kayla nodded albeit a bit grimly. "She's in there, somewhere. Thankfully she's not the clawing type. We'll find her."

Maddie looked from Kayla to Elsa and realized that she didn't believe them. She didn't know what was going on, but…it wasn't a cat. Or a missing dress.

The question was whether to demand to see the cat and get to the bottom of this, or simply leave as they so obviously wanted her to do?

"Tell me the truth," she said to Kayla. "There wasn't a dye explosion or anything in that room? All the new dresses are—"

"Everything is fine," Kayla assured her. "Elsa almost had the cat out when you came in. I'm sure she'll get her this time. Thankfully all the dresses are in bags, so it isn't like she'll be able to do some serious damage to tulle and lace."

"Yes," Maddie agreed. "That is something to be grateful for."

"I'm sorry that you have to work on Danna's dress during what has to be a difficult time," Kayla said in a voice that made Maddie want to believe everything was all right.

"It's fine. Life goes on." Maddie bounced a look between her partner and her partner's niece, then decided she really didn't care. She was on leave from the business. Kayla was dependable and had her back. There might or might not be a cat in the back room, but she was going to give them the benefit of the doubt.

"All right. If you'd drop that dress by Ashley's, I'll make arrangements to discuss it with her later."

"Will do. I promise. And, Maddie…honest to goodness, that's the only stock I've ever taken out of the place."

"You own half of it," Maddie said. "No biggie." And they had no rules about what happened to old stock they couldn't sell. Usually a deep discount did the trick with the samples, but every now and again they had a dress that refused to leave. Once before, Maddie and Ashley had used one as a base for a collaboration, and she hoped to do it again with the dress Kayla had taken home. "I have a meeting with Holly at the café," she said simply. "I'll be in touch."

She and Sean had driven to town together that morning, he to shop for miscellaneous items he and Dillon needed to fix the damaged truck and she to deal with Danna's dress and touch base with Holly about catering the open house. The dress part was done, now the other, then she could escape back to the ranch.

Kayla and Elsa stood side by side, smiling as Maddie opened the front door, forgetting her promise to herself to exit via the back. She gritted her teeth as the wedding march chimes sounded then stepped outside into the brisk December air. There was definitely something weird going on in the shop. It felt a lot like the surprise birthday party Kayla had thrown for her a few years ago, but her birthday wasn't for six months.

Maybe they were hiding a gushing bride, she mused as she walked down the street to meet Sean at the truck. Or there might really be a cat. Maybe she was simply too ready to look for signs of trouble when there were none. With the exception of Sean, that was.

She might well be dabbling with trouble there, but right now, she felt as if they were two survivors negotiating post-disaster waters together. Their waters were different, his having to do with a rodeo wreck and hers with a nuptial wreck, but they understood one another. And while Maddie knew it would sting when they parted ways if she became too dependent on having a sympathetic ear, it wouldn't come close to the sting of being dumped after a sixteen-month engagement.

"I'm glad to see you looking more like yourself," Holly said as she closed the folder which held the catering sheet they'd just gone over. Everything was in order. Holly promised that her daughter and daughter-in-law would be at the guest ranch early Saturday afternoon and would stay until the open house was over at nine that evening. They were old hands at catering, thus freeing Maddie up to smile and make small talk with guests.

"I'm feeling more like myself," Maddie

said. She had a strong urge to tell Holly that she was beginning to see that Cody had saved them from a huge mistake, but resisted. Not that Holly would tell anyone if she was asked not to. "Life goes on."

"Good for you, honey." Holly glanced around the room, checking her customers, then up at the clock before setting a hand on the glass countertop. "You should know that Cody's been coming in for take-out almost every day."

"Is that a warning?"

"It is getting close to that time, and I wasn't sure if—"

"I'd rather not bump into him." It was going to happen, as it already had on the ranch, but she wasn't going to court trouble.

"It might take a bit before you're ready to randomly run into the man," Holly said sympathetically.

Maddie nodded, but the truth was that awkwardness was more of a concern than the pain of seeing the man who'd come to realize he didn't love her.

"Thanks for everything, Holly. I truly appreciate it. I don't think I could have come up with enough finger food to handle an open house."

"Nor would Shirl expect you to." Holly beamed at her. "You take care now, hon."

Maddie was doing her best in that regard, and honestly, she thought she was doing okay.

After she left the café, she resisted the urge to pop back into Spurs and Veils to see if they'd found the cat. She'd work with Ashley on the dress for Danna, but other than that, she needn't have any bridal shop–related thoughts at all.

And she wouldn't be, if Kayla and Elsa hadn't acted so darned odd.

"Arteaga!"

Sean turned to see a man approaching him with determined strides. It took him a minute to place him and when he did, he wished he hadn't. Mitch Dietrich, the brother of the advertising director of one of Sean's sponsors, with whom Sean was loosely acquainted.

"Mitch."

"I'd heard that you were in the area, and you, sir, could quite possibly be the miracle I need."

"I'm not feeling very miraculous at the moment."

Mitch laughed and flashed his white teeth. "Don't be modest."

Mitch was good-looking, not superbright in an academic sense, but coyote smart. The guy could see an angle. Fortunately he'd married the daughter of a local bigwig, and she kept him from starting random pyramid schemes in his spare time.

"Mindy's dad is the chair for the Christmas event this year, and the grand marshal of our parade had to bow out. This year's theme is 'Cowboy Christmas,' and I can't think of a better representative than you."

"That desperate?"

"I have two days to find someone. The parade is this Saturday."

"Here's the thing." Sean tipped his face so that Mitch got the full effect of the still-angry scars. "I don't feel qualified to be the face of anything."

Mitch, who'd never been good at hiding

his feelings, grimaced, reminding Sean of when Maddie had told him that he wasn't pretty anymore.

"I'm not there yet."

"Where?"

"To the point that I can lead a parade and have people gawk at me."

"People appreciate a warrior," Mitch said. When Sean showed no sign of relenting, he added, "Chicks dig scars?"

"It's not for me. Sorry." He pulled out the fob and unlocked his truck.

"Arteaga…"

"Sorry."

Mitch was a guy used to getting his way, and now that he was an important part of the community, he probably was batting close to a thousand in that regard.

Sean opened his door, then looked to where Mitch was still standing near the curb, as if expecting Sean to come to his senses at any minute. "I'm sure you'll find a cowboy to lead your parade."

"This is an honor, Arteaga."

"I don't feel qualified."

He wasn't a hometown hero. He was

simply a guy with a somewhat recognizable name if one followed rodeo.

"Hey," he said as Mitch gave him a "your loss" look. "I appreciate the ask."

Even if it was out of desperation.

He headed toward his truck while Mitch took off in the opposite direction, still in search of his cowboy grand marshal, then slowed his pace when he heard footsteps hurrying behind him. It was kind of crazy that he recognized those footsteps. How?

Maybe because he'd been thinking about Maddie and he assumed that she might be catching up with him, which she was.

"Hey," she said, a little puff of crystalline breath accompanying her words.

"Hey." He didn't ask if she was okay being in town because he'd asked that too many times already. Nothing in his rather solitary life had prepared him to deal with the pain of others. He was kind of at a loss, and decided to go with his gut instead of trying to follow a script that seemed right, but wasn't working.

Want to get a beer? his gut asked, so he spoke the words aloud.

"Yes."

The instant and heartfelt reply surprised him as did the fact that she clutched his coat when her foot skidded on an icy patch. She let go as soon as she regained her balance, but he held out his arm and Maddie shot him a quick look before putting her hand back on it.

"Safer when you're wearing sissy shoes."

"These aren't sissy shoes. The sidewalk has not been properly shoveled."

He had to agree, but since the snow only stopped falling half an hour ago, he'd give the store owners a pass.

They ducked into the Hickory Pub, a microbrewery that boasted a food counter, and picked a high top in the corner.

"Do you really want beer?" Sean asked, thinking she might have simply wanted to find an out of the way place to sit for a bit.

"Yes. Dark."

"You got it."

A few minutes later he returned with one dark beer and one nonalcoholic ale. With snow on top of ice, he wasn't taking chances with his reflexes. His luck hadn't been running so good lately, and he didn't want to push things.

When he got to the table, Maddie was peering out the window in the direction of her bridal shop. She lifted the heavy glass mug, took a long drink, and when she set the glass down, she had a foam mustache. She wiped the moisture off with her thumb.

"Look at us," she said matter-of-factly.

"How so?"

"Sharing an afternoon beer when not that long ago, I might have crossed the street if I'd seen you coming."

He liked down-to-earth, snarky Maddie. "Where was this dark side of you back in the day?"

"Living in some unacknowledged part of my brain?"

He gave her a wry look. "A little of your optimism might have rubbed off on me."

"How much?" she asked suspiciously.

He held up his hand with his thumb and forefinger a couple of millimeters apart.

"That much?" Maddie said in mock awe.

He gave a solemn nod and was rewarded with a crooked smile that kind of lit him up inside. But the smile faded, and she reached for her beer and drank as if she needed to forget.

"Is everything okay?" he asked.

"I don't know." She wiped the moisture off her lower lip and his gaze followed the movement before he realized what he was doing. "The vibe was off in my shop."

"How so?"

"Kayla and Elsa were acting strange. They said that there was a cat loose in the vault, but…"

"Wait. You have a vault?"

"A storage room. Lots of money tied up in dresses there, so we call it the vault. Elsa supposedly brought her cat to work so she could take it to the vet, but it got loose."

"And you don't believe them?"

Maddie glanced at her beer glass, turned it in her hands, then looked back up again. "It wasn't the first excuse they came up with to keep me out of the back."

"What do you think…?"

"I don't know. What could it be?"

Sean put the flat of his hand on the table. "Let's go see."

"Really?"

"If it's going to bother you, yes."

Confronted with the possibility of discovering her boogeyman, Maddie relaxed.

"It's going to bother me, but…should I let it? I'm on leave. I'm not even supposed to be there. If they have some kind of emergency that they don't want me to know about… then I guess I'll let it go." She drank again, in a way that made Sean glad that he was driving. "I'll tell you a secret," she said, glancing sideways as if to see if anyone was nearby, "I'm tired of weddings. Prom season is so much more fun for me. And this isn't the jilted bride speaking."

"You've been thinking about it for a while, then?"

She met his gaze dead on. "No, Sean. I've been *not* thinking about it. Not admitting it to myself. I guess my dealings with Cody are causing me to look at things more honestly. I'm good at my job, but…brides?" She placed her forearms on the table. "The business is lucrative. We get customers from all over the area. I think they like coming to a quaint little out-of-the-way shop and we're good at what we do."

"I bet you are."

She sighed and picked up the napkin next to her beer, made a few accordion pleats, then set it on the table, watching as it unfurled itself.

"Maybe this *is* the jilted bride speaking. Or maybe I'm just tired because of everything that's happened. I'll muscle through and by this time next year, I'm sure I'll be happily helping brides choose dresses for June weddings." He lifted his eyebrows and she said, "It takes at least six months to get a dress made and fitted. I prefer that the bride gives me a year. That helps head off all sorts of disasters."

"Like?"

"Production problems. Fitting problems. Lost-in-transit problems. A lot of these dresses are made overseas, and the shipping can be a nail-biter."

"Wow."

"Yeah." She reached for her beer, took another drink, then pushed it to the side, still half-full.

"Done?"

"Maybe so." She smiled. "I like the idea of having a day drink, but apparently I'm not good at it."

"Then it's time to go." Sean left his seat to pay at the bar, and Maddie met him at the door. As they walked to the truck, she said musingly, "This is strange."

"What?"

"Me confessing my job fatigue."

"Why? I'm the perfect guy to confess to, because I'm not going to tell you to look at the—"

She smacked his shoulder and he winced and laughed. Maddie gave him an exasperated look, then slipped and would have gone down if he hadn't hauled her back onto her feet. Now she laughed as she bumped against him and he put his arms around her, on the Main Street sidewalk for all to see.

"Thank you. I have this." She stepped back and opened her hands with a flourish as if to demonstrate how balanced she was as she stood next to the icy patch on the sidewalk that had almost been her undoing.

Despite her perfect balance, Sean offered his arm, and she took it. A few steps later her hand casually dropped from his arm and a whisper of regret went through him.

He wasn't going to think about whispers of regret or what they might mean because...because he didn't want to. Instead he wanted to enjoy the company of the woman walking beside him, keeping an eye out for more slick spots. Their time together was limited, so why not enjoy it?

"Maddie."

She shot him a sideways look, frowning at his businesslike tone. But businesslike was the tone he needed to keep her from retreating, as she might well do after she heard him out.

"Wanna have some Christmas fun?"

She gave him a curious look. "As if we haven't had enough of that already?"

"I admit that we're getting close to the saturation point, but we're not there yet."

"What do you propose?"

He had a few ideas involving mistletoe and the like, but instead he gestured toward the sign in the bank window, advertising the Giving Tree gift program.

"Dillon's Leadership Club runs that event. Want to shop for some kids?"

Her smile made him feel ridiculously lighthearted.

"I like it," she said. "Let's do it."

CHAPTER ELEVEN

"I THINK YOU have train envy," Maddie said as they left Larkspur's business center, which housed a toy store in the basement. She could think of no other reason for her partner in Christmas cheer to be smiling with so much satisfaction as they left the store basement.

"Not going to argue that point." He patted the box he carried under his arm. "This is a great set."

"You might be going a touch over budget…"

"Which is why I chose to buy for brothers. I'm totally on budget for two kids."

The Giving Tree was arranged so that the giver could opt to buy for an individual child or for a family. Sean had chosen a family of two boys, while Maddie had chosen two teen girls, intending to head to Eva's Emporium.

"Do you mind if I leave you to it?" he asked after setting the train set in the back seat of his truck.

"I will not ask you to shop for teen clothing." She, on the other hand, was looking forward to some fun. Bright colors, fun fashion. Things she hadn't indulged in for some time.

"I'll make it up to you."

She stopped next to his truck, tilting her head as she asked, "How are you going to do that?"

He flashed his teeth in a pirate smile and Maddie's breath hitched. Why didn't he do that more often?

Because it wouldn't be good for you, her small voice assured her. She had to agree. Even Cody had never had the power to dazzle her senses the way Sean could. But dazzle didn't hold up day to day. If was fun for the interim; the interlude between one reality and the next. What would her next reality look like?

"I'll come up with something."

"That's not very reassuring," she said with a frown. "You look like you're hatching a plot."

"A Christmas plot? Perhaps I am." He gave a low *mwah-ha-ha* and twirled an invisible mustache.

She mock scowled and he laughed for real, lifting a hand to touch her cheek. The feeling of his warm palm against her skin in the crisp air was reassuring. Someone had her back. Someone who had no reason to lie to her, and she could not shake the feeling that Kayla and Elsa were not exactly lying, but hiding something from her. Had a pipe broken in the vault?

"Maddie, Maddie," Sean said softly, looking at her as if trying to solve a puzzle, seemingly unaware that they were on a public street with Christmas music playing from a speaker over their heads. Something had shifted, and she needed to put them back on track. Now. Before she gave in to temptation here in public and the jilted bride and the scarred-up bronc rider were seen kissing on the street. It was one thing to kiss at the lodge, another to do it in public, where word would certainly get back to Dillon. And Cody—not that that mattered, but she had to admit it would be satisfying.

"What do you want for Christmas?" she asked.

The words had the effect she'd hoped for; he scowled and dropped his hand.

"Do not buy me a gift."

She held his gaze. "Likewise."

"I'm serious."

"Me, too." She took a backward step, feeling more herself as she widened the space between them. She had to widen it, or she might have kissed the man before he kissed her. In the public parking lot behind the business center.

Just because.

DILLON ARRIVED HOME at the lodge stoked because his team had taken first in the tournament. He'd won his match, but it was a squeaker—his words—and he needed to up his game. Sean and Maddie had listened to a blow by blow of the match, complete with wrestling pantomime, as they wrapped the Christmas presents for the Giving Tree kids. Despite Dillon's enthusiastic replay of his match, Sean sensed that something was off. He didn't know what gave him that impression, and he didn't know if Maddie noticed, but decided that when he and Dillon worked on the truck the next day, he'd give the kid an opening to talk.

"So there you go," Dillon said as he finished his narrative with a flourish. "Champions."

"Congratulations," Maddie said as she took the tape from Sean, their fingers brushing in the process. Strange how such a small thing could feel intimate, and Sean wondered if he needed to be concerned. Not for Maddie, but for himself.

He'd fallen hard twice in his life. Messed up twice. He wasn't down for a repeat performance. But Maddie seemed to be negotiating the new aspects of their relationship with relative ease.

Because she sees it for what it is.

She'd been honest, and he'd been kind of honest. He fully intended to simply enjoy her company, no expectations, because she didn't want or need anything in that regard, nor did he, but he couldn't help feeling that he was sliding closer to the abyss.

That wouldn't be good for either of them.

But when Maddie glanced up at him, a smile in her eyes, before turning her attention to Dillon, he felt a wallop of need.

You are a rebound guy. A temporary port in a storm.

They'd share some laughs, enjoy some kisses, move on, better because of the interlude, but understanding exactly what it had been.

They hadn't said the words aloud, but the situation was obvious. They were helping each other through a transition phase. Their ultimate destinations were miles apart. He'd be heading off to school, learning his trade; in fact, he'd called Finn that afternoon to tell him not to bother setting up the interview with Snow Crest Ranch. That he was very appreciative but had managed to secure a spot in his training program. Maddie would recover from the curveball life had thrown her and probably continue with her bridal shop business as before. Or perhaps she'd get out of the wedding game and try something new as she'd hinted at when they'd had their beer.

The moral of the story—he needed to get

a grip. Enjoy their time together. Move on when the time came.

"A penny for them," Maddie murmured after Dillon had drifted away to attend to an important phone call from a friend.

"I was thinking about the future."

She lifted her eyebrows politely, but he merely shrugged as he put ribbon around the wrapped train set. Silence was one of his strengths and he employed it automatically without feeling one bit self-conscious. He found that if he remained silent while people yammered on, they often went away. Not that Maddie was yammering or that he wanted her to go away. He just wanted to talk about other matters.

"Nothing more?"

He shook his head as he concentrated on curling ribbon. When he was done, he set down the scissors and found her studying him. "Nothing concrete," he said.

"Just random future thoughts?"

"Yeah."

Her lips curved into a smile that brought out the small crease in her cheek that he found so fascinating. When had Maddie developed the ability to fascinate him?

Years ago, actually. When she wasn't engaging him in optimistic conversation, which had put his back up, he'd found her take on life both fascinating and foreign. He'd deemed it unrealistic, and looking back, he hadn't been far off base there, but it had been hard not to be affected by her innate cheerfulness.

The fascination he felt now was different, more rooted in reality, as was Maddie.

"Sean?"

He glanced up, realized he'd missed a question. "Hmm?"

She stacked one of her packages on top of the other, offsetting them so as not to crush the bows. "Do you think everything is okay with Dillon?"

"I'll find out when we work on the truck."

"You think that something was off, too?"

"He seemed distracted."

"Good." He frowned and she said, "Not that I want him to be distracted. I'm wondering about my intuition. I missed the mark with Cody and now I think I might be looking for signs that aren't there. Kayla and Elsa at the shop. Dillon."

"He was not his usual self."

Maddie gave a slow nod. "Then I'm going to believe that my intuition is correct in both cases. There was something off at the shop, and I'm going to find out what it is."

"What could it be?"

"That's what has me puzzled. I can't think of a thing."

"Maybe it's a good thing? A…surprise?"

Lame, but maybe…? Like Maddie, he had a hard time thinking of what a bridal shop secret might be.

"Mmm," she said with a wry smile. "Like that time you surprised me?"

He drew in a breath at the reference to their first kiss. "Maybe?"

"Wanna surprise me again?"

He put his hands on her shoulders, thinking that he'd like nothing better, but…

"What?" she asked softly. "Is there a problem?"

Any doubts Maddie had about her intuition could be laid to rest. She was reading him like a book.

He dropped his hands, but stayed where he was, standing mere inches away from her. "You know that these…surprises…are leading nowhere, right?"

She took a step back, turning the inches between them into feet. At least two,

Very smooth Arteaga. He put a hand on the back of his neck and squeezed. "That didn't come out the way I intended."

"It's okay," Maddie said softly. "I know what you're saying. I don't want to take advantage of you."

"What? No. I—"

She lifted an eyebrow and he stopped.

Then he tried again. "Look. I'm not good at this. I'm a guy who in the end goes it alone."

"Are you telling me not to get my hopes up?"

No. I'm telling me *not to get my hopes up.*

Maddie searched his face, looking for an answer he didn't think she would find, but then she nodded as if coming to a conclusion.

"You are," she said.

"No." The single word seemed to work.

Good. He didn't have a lot of words at the moment.

He reached for her hands, and to his surprise, instead of resisting the contact, she let him take them. But she did not allow him to speak first.

"You're overthinking, Sean. I can use an ally. You're it."

He wasn't an overthinker. That was what touchy-feely people did and he was not one of those. But he couldn't deny the wave of relief that washed over him when she'd said she needed an ally.

"I screwed this up."

Maddie gave him a gentle smirk. "Does this mean no more surprises?"

He smiled. "I can probably come up with something." He squeezed her fingers as he pulled her a step closer, then nearly jumped out of his skin when Dillon coughed from behind them.

The kid had obviously caught them holding hands and prepping for more, but he made a show of nonchalance as Sean and Maddie dropped hands and eased apart. Maddie ran a hand over her hair and then rearranged the stacked gifts on the table next to them, while Sean said, "I guess we'll get started on that radiator early tomorrow."

"Sounds good," Dillon said briskly, not quite meeting his eyes. "Anyone seen my— There it is." He went to the end table and picked up his tablet. "Well…" he bobbed his head "…carry on."

Maddie wrinkled her forehead as she watched him disappear down the hall, then said, "I might just run along myself."

"Me, too," Sean replied. "I have a saddle that needs cleaned."

SEAN AND DILLON tackled the radiator replacement immediately after breakfast the next day. Dillon had read up on the matter, and so Sean let the kid direct the operation, only stepping in when needed.

After pulling the wrecked radiator off the frame, Dillon said, "You didn't want to be grand marshal of the Christmas parade?"

Sean, who'd been wondering how to nudge the kid toward talking about what had been bugging him the day before, now found himself on the defensive.

"How do you know that?" Sean asked.

"Locker room gossip," Dillon said off-handedly.

Locker rooms had changed since he'd played basketball back in the day.

"Carl's Uncle Mitch is in charge." Dillon shot him a look. "Why didn't you want to do it? I mean, you've been in magazines."

"Not many." But the ads had been lucrative, which was why he had the money he needed for his schooling.

Dillon didn't answer and Sean eventually said, "I don't like being the center of attention unless there's a bronc involved." Total truth.

"Or felt sorry for? You know, because of your scar."

"Not a fan," Sean replied, although he'd disliked attention prior to the accident. Posing for photographs was different from interacting with fans. He was grateful for those fans, but never felt like he had enough to give back in return for their support. "I don't know if it's pride or ego."

"Both, I imagine." Dillon spoke as if there was no question about it and Sean had to admit the kid was right. Pride and ego. Where did one stop and the other start?

"We have this kid on the team who lost his hand in a baling accident," Dillon continued. "He does good. Goes out onto the mat and shows them who's boss."

Sean gave the kid a sideways look. "That takes courage."

"Manuel has been living with his injury since seventh grade. He's used to it."

Indicating that Sean was still coming to terms, which he was, although he no longer felt impatient with himself when tasks took longer than they once did. And he'd gotten used to the scars on his face. He just hated being stared at.

"That's impressive," Sean said, regarding Dillon's teammate.

"Yeah. He has a girlfriend and everything. It's all about attitude."

"Do you have a girlfriend?" Sean asked curiously.

"Do you?" Dillon shot back.

He'd touched the sore spot. Girl trouble. "You want to talk?"

"Not especially," Dillon said. "I'll figure things out."

Sean gave Dillon a hand placing the new radiator in place, thinking the talk was over. Dillon wasn't ready to spill, and now that Sean knew what the deal was, he could relax.

Once the bolts were in, Dillon stepped back, surveying their work. He didn't look at Sean as he said, "The question is, will you?"

"Will I what?"

"Figure things out." Dillon faked a cough as he said, "Maddie."

"Not happening."

"Then who was that woman you were holding hands with last night?"

"That was nothing."

"You can plead the fifth, you know, but I think you guys are kind of cute." Dillon held up his hands as Sean scowled at him. "It's not my business, so I'll butt out."

"There's nothing going on between us. Maddie's still getting over her broken engagement." Dillon merely shrugged, so

Sean decided to give the kid a dose of reality. "I was engaged twice before myself." Actually officially only once, but he'd been about to ask when Shay dumped him. "Both times they blew up. Totally my fault. I'm not going there again."

Dillon cocked his head, considered for a moment, then said, "Maybe they weren't the ones."

The kid gave him a "so there" look and before Sean could formulate an answer, the teen crossed the bay to the box holding the new grill, which had cost an exorbitant amount of money, considering the fact that it was plastic. He started unwrapping the protective padding as if unaware that he'd just executed a mic drop.

Sean joined him at the grill, carting the protective wrap to the pile of packaging next to the bay door, then returning to help Dillon carry the new grill to the truck.

They set down the grill and Sean straightened. "Maybe I'll call Mitch and see if he's still looking for a cowboy to lead the Christmas parade."

It was the only thing he could think of

to distract the kid from a topic he'd been foolish to broach. Girlfriends. And surely Mitch had someone by now, so it would simply be a courtesy call.

Dillon gave him a sly sideways look. "He is. I told him I'd see if I could talk you into it."

"Do you need anything from town?" Maddie stood on the lower tractor step and spoke to Sean through the open door over the noise of the engine.

"Not that I can think of," he said.

There'd been a shift in their dynamic since he'd made certain that she understood his need to "go it alone" and Dillon had caught them holding hands. She was now the one creating the distance, and thankfully he was following her lead. She did not want him to think for one minute that she was pining for him, or that kissing him was anything more than pleasant. That would destroy the fragile bond they'd built, and she found that she needed that bond at this point in time. She hadn't been kidding about needing an ally. Plus, it would hurt her pride for him to think that she was taking things more seriously than he was.

She was a jilted bride for Pete's sake. She was simply getting her sea legs back. Building confidence, things like that. He was the guy who knew what she was going through. Surely, he understood that.

Do you?

Her little voice was becoming irksome.

"You're *only* going to the store?" Sean asked in a seemingly offhand way, but she heard the cautionary note to his voice.

Instead of answering, she gave a tight-lipped smile and then descended the tractor steps. She planned to have a chat with Kayla both to see if they found the possibly imaginary cat, and to test if her spider senses were still tingling. It was possible that she'd simply misread the situation. That, like Sean, she'd been overthinking.

"Maddie," Sean said as she was about to close the door.

"What?"

He let out a breath, as if realizing that he wanted to say something neither of them wanted to hear. The guy was protective, even of those he didn't want to get too close to.

Or he is afraid of getting too close to, just like you are.

She'd pushed that thought out of her brain more than once, and she did so again as she said, "I'm dropping the presents at the bank for the Giving Tree, then going to the store."

The bridal store.

Then, in case he had more questions that she didn't want to answer, she said, "Sean… you know that you have no say in what I do."

"Of course I don't." He practically sputtered the words.

"Just checking." She was doing more than that. She was making a point. He wasn't the only one going it alone.

He gave her a stony nod, she shut the tractor door and then headed across the driveway to her idling truck. It was ridiculous that asserting their independence from one another made her feel closer to the man. It shouldn't work that way.

She had a feeling that she'd just fixed things so that there would be no more surprise kisses, which was probably best in the long run. They shouldn't have set off down that track to begin with.

Because if they hadn't, she probably wouldn't be having the disconcerting experience of having Sean Arteaga shove his way into her dreams, making her want things she wasn't ready to have.

CHAPTER TWELVE

MITCH HAD BEEN glad to receive Sean's call, saying that he would be happy to lead the Christmas parade, scars and all. After Mitch had expressed his thanks, he'd imparted good news and bad. The good news was that Sean didn't have to show up for any kind of an orientation meeting or practice. The bad was that he had to wear a cowboy Santa suit and needed to try it on.

"The organizers are going to be stoked," Mitch said. "You're a name, you know. People will come out to see you."

Sean thought people would be more likely to come out because it was Christmas, although he had signed his fair share of autographs back in the day. He was no longer a bronc rider, though, and people had no reason to want to see him. But if Mitch wanted to believe that people were going to come out for him rather than Santa, he wasn't going to dissuade the man.

"We need to meet and see if the costume fits you," Mitch said. "I'm sure it will, but just in case…you know."

Sean had to go to town to see about wiring his tuition payment to the MDMI bursar, so he promised to meet with Mitch then.

"Sounds good, buddy. Thanks."

"Yeah."

In the broad scheme of things, having to play Santa was no big deal. The bigger deal, which he was still having some difficulty wrapping his mind around, was the fact that as soon as he sent the tuition money, he was officially a student again. Things had worked out. Again, his only concern was the promise he'd made to Max, but the man had assured him via text, that he had no qualms about leaving the place in Maddie's hands with Dillon there to help.

Things had worked out. Sean was free to go on his way.

To go it alone, he thought with a smirk as he entered his cabin and shrugged out of his coat.

He'd just pulled his arm out of the sleeve when a motion caught his eye. He went to the window and saw the wind blow the rear door of the stock trailer open a few inches, then bang it shut. It hadn't been properly latched.

He left his hat and gloves on the table and let himself out of the cabin, crossing the driveway, which he'd plowed after the last snow, to the trailer. He caught the door as it blew open and then noticed that there was something inside toward the front. The packing material from the radiator, bumper and grill. Dillon must have put it there to keep until the next run to the dump, which made sense. It wasn't cluttering up the barn and it wasn't underfoot elsewhere.

He ran his hands over his arms, started to close the trailer, then stopped. The big slab of cardboard would be perfect to set the saddles on while he soaped and oiled them, thus keeping him from constantly cleaning the floor when he was done with one saddle and about to begin on the next. He let himself into the trailer and crossed to the tangle of shrink-wrap, bubble wrap, foam and cardboard. He'd just found the perfect piece when a gust of wind hit the trailer, buffeting it hard. The door slammed shut, rattling the interior and making Sean's ears ring.

Clutching the cardboard, he made his way back to the door and pushed.

Then pushed again. Finally he gave it a desperate rattle. The door did not budge.

He leaned a forearm on the solid door, and let his forehead fall forward onto his jacket sleeve. Really?

He'd heard of this happening, but...really? The impact of the trailer door slamming in the wind had knocked the latch loose and it had dropped into place. Sean banged his palm on the metal door, then blew out a breath and considered options.

Freezing to death?

At least he was wearing his coat. And Maddie would be home soon.

He hoped.

He rattled the door again, then when that did no good, took hold of the supports near the open area at the top and pulled himself up to see if he could find a solution.

There was no way he could reach the

latch, even if he could keep himself off the ground and get his arm through the space.

Slowly he slid back down the wall of the trailer. Someone would be home before dark. They'd let him out. He'd be embarrassed, but at least he wouldn't freeze to death.

But why, why, why hadn't he grabbed his hat and gloves? It was going to be a freaking cold wait for rescue. He sat down on the pile, which shifted beneath his weight.

Was fate trying to make a point? To show him that he couldn't always go it alone? That sometimes he needed to be rescued?

He wasn't having it.

He got to his feet and started picking up bits of material. The cardboard would do no good. The bubble wrap…no. The shrink-wrap? Maybe.

He took a length of the wrap and twisted it into something loosely resembling a rope, then hefted himself back up to where he could see out of the twelve-inch open gap between the trailer walls and roof. He considered the gap, decided he'd rather not get stuck and instead dangled the loop outside, trying to hook the handle.

The cold metal stung his hands and his cheek where he'd pressed it against the opening to allow more of his arm to hang out. He made several desperate passes with the loop to no avail. He pulled in the loop, went back to the stash, knotted another length of shrink-wrap onto the first, then tried again.

Third time was a charm. He caught the latch, slowly lifted. The loop slipped off the handle, but the next time he tried, the latch popped free.

Yes! He was the man.

Feeling cocky, and relieved that he didn't need a rescue, Sean tossed the shrink-wrap loop back onto the pile of packing material, picked up his cardboard and stepped out of the trailer a cold weary champion. He'd gone it alone, and he'd beat the odds.

He latched the door, picked up the cardboard, caught the heel of his boot on a frozen rock and went down hard. His cheekbone smashed into the frozen ground and for a moment he lay there, catching his breath, shock preventing him from feeling the pain that he knew would soon arrive. He pushed himself up to his hands and knees and then to his feet.

When he stood, his head swam, but he still bent to pick up the cardboard. He'd almost done himself in getting the stuff and he was darned well going to bring it with him.

And then he half limped, half stumbled to his cabin as the world swam around him.

MADDIE JUGGLED HER keys until she found the one that opened the back door of Spurs and Veils. She was moving forward with her life in a serious way—thank you, Sean—but was not yet ready to hear the cheery bars of the wedding march that played when the front door opened. When she came back to work, she was going to discuss changing the tune to something else. Surely, they could find something romantic, yet not traumatizing to possible jilted brides?

Or maybe you can put on your big girl panties and own up to reality. Because she'd decided in the early hours of the morning, she would be coming back to work when her six-week leave was up. She might not tackle her job with the same joy, but she would eventually get her mojo back.

Reality was starting to feel better all the time. She would get through this and come out the other side stronger than before.

Maddie eased the heavy steel door open and was about to call out, so as not to scare the daylights out of Elsa and Kayla, when she heard the low rumble of a male voice. A potential groom?

If so, what was he doing in their small break room, where they kept the coffee, a minifridge and the flower cooler?

Clutching her purse a little tighter, Maddie quietly crossed to where she could see into the room, then swallowed dryly as she saw a very, as in *very*, familiar cowboy hat sitting on the table. The same hat that she'd given Cody for Christmas last year. The 50X hat that had eaten a major hole in her budget.

She couldn't see anyone, but she could hear Kayla's voice murmuring something low and intimate, followed by Cody giving a low laugh, and then Kayla sighing.

Rooted to the floor, her cheeks ablaze, Maddie listened to the unmistakable sounds of two people kissing. At least she hoped that was all she was listening to.

Get out of here! Now!

Maddie needed no convincing. She had the presence of mind to make sure she had a clear path to the back door and turned carefully in the crowded staging area so as not to knock anything over and call attention to herself.

The floorboards creaked under her feet, but neither Kayla nor Cody seemed to hear. She was almost to the exit, feeling like she was about to jump out of her skin, when the door leading to the front sales area opened, and Elsa appeared.

"Maddie," she said on a gasp.

A small crash came from the break room, then Kayla appeared in the doorway, pushing her mussed blond hair back into place. She pasted on a wide super fake smile. "We didn't expect to see you until after Christmas."

"Obviously." Maddie tilted her chin up, giving her business partner a look that probably defied description—a proper reflection of her feelings, which also defied description. "How long?"

"I don't understand what you mean." Kayla said in a convincingly innocent voice. Elsa ruined it by dropping her gaze in a guilt-by-association way.

"Maybe Cody can explain it to you," Maddie said, gesturing toward the break room with her chin. "How long?"

That was when Cody appeared in the doorway behind Kayla, and set a hand on her shoulder.

Kayla said, "Two weeks," in a grudging voice at the same time that Cody said, "Since the Labor Day Rodeo."

Kayla shot him a killer look, but Cody pretended not to see.

"Which is it?" Maddie said to her business partner, who was now red to her hairline.

"We didn't kiss until two weeks ago." One look at Cody told Maddie that was also a lie.

"I see." Her voice was stone. Her body was stone. How was she going to get it to move so that she could escape this nightmare?

Cody stepped in front of Kayla. "Can we talk outside?"

"My question has been answered" was all Maddie said. Her legs finally responded to her brain, and she started across the storage area to the back door.

"Maddie."

Blood pounded in her ears, making it impossible to tell who'd said her name, or maybe her brain was so scrambled that it was short-circuiting. But there was no mistaking the voice she heard once she broke free of the boutique and stepped into the alley.

"Maddie," Cody said again.

She kept moving, caught her toe on a crack in the pavement and took a few drunken steps in an effort to retain her balance. By the time she'd regained her footing, Cody was in front of her.

"We didn't do anything until after you and I broke up."

"Liar." She tested the word and got the result she'd expected. He went even redder.

Maddie stared up at him for a long moment, wanting very much to rage at him; but more than that, she wanted to rage at Kayla. Her trusted partner. Scratch the *trusted* part.

"Leave. Me. Alone."

With that she turned on her heel and marched unseeingly down the alley. She heard the sound of boots on asphalt, turned and held up her hand in a "stop" motion. "Go comfort Kayla. I'm sure she needs it."

"Maddie."

"If you follow me, I'll make a lot of noise and Christmas shoppers will come to my rescue." Indeed, people were already sending curious looks into the alley as they walked past, packages and bags in hand.

She lifted her chin as if to ascertain that he understood, then turned and marched out of the alley to the parking lot where she'd managed to find a spot for her truck not that long ago.

It was only when she was inside and had the engine running that she let the tears fall.

Her business partner had cheated on her.

MADDIE DID NOT start her truck immediately, because she was too upset to drive on slick roads. Instead she sat behind her steering wheel brushing away tears that refused to stop falling.

And then they did. Maddie wiped at her face as her head cleared.

A cheerful chime announced a text. Kayla. Maddie dropped her phone as if it were infected.

She leaned against the headrest, watching people wearing heavy winter coats drifting down the sidewalk, popping in and out of stores.

Another chime.

Maddie ignored it, settling an elbow on the window frame next to her and propping her head on her hand. What now?

Run and hide? Let this eat at you?

Sort it out? How would she sort this out?

Run and hide sounded good. She started to turn the key, then stopped when she caught sight of Cody making his way down the sidewalk in front of the parking lot, oblivious to the fact that she was watching.

She felt nothing for the man. Nothing good, anyway. But...she couldn't bring herself to say she hated him. That was close enough to nothing to convince her she had indeed dodged a bullet. If he'd fallen for some-one else, well that was maybe meant to be.

But the lying.

She closed her eyes and leaned her head back again. Cody lied. Kayla lied. Elsa was an accessory.

Her phone chimed again. She opened her eyes in time to see Cody's truck drive past the parking lot, then without letting herself consider anything close to consequences, she shoved her door open, remembered to grab the keys out of the ignition at the last second, then headed across the lot to Spurs and Veils.

Only this time she let herself in the front door, ignored the happy chimes and stopped in the middle of the floor. Kayla appeared out of the back, then stopped dead.

"Maddie. I don't know what to say." Her gaze darted past Maddie to the door as if hoping for a rescue. Or maybe an escape, but Maddie had that route blocked.

"Then I'll ask questions and you answer."

"There was a vibe, Maddie. We ignored it for the longest time. For you."

"Until?" Maddie prompted. Her voice was hard, and she liked the sound of it.

"Labor Day. I had a flat tire. Cody helped me fix it. He'd come here to see you, but you were in Bozeman meeting with that client, and…" She gave Maddie a "do you really want to hear this" look. "Nothing happened…really."

Maddie knew Kayla's mannerisms and was certain she was not being truthful. She'd seen the same look when a bride insisted on an unflattering dress and Kayla, reading the moment, would confirm that it was the perfect dress for her. After all, she and Maddie had agreed, it wasn't their big day and if the bride and her entourage liked a particular dress, then they should have it.

Kayla angled her chin, as if daring Maddie to contradict her. Maddie saw no sense in doing that. She had to work with this woman until she figured a way out, and she was going to.

"I'm going to find a buyer for my half of the store."

Kayla pursed her lips together. "I don't want to work with a stranger."

"But you will work with the woman with whose fiancé you cheated?"

"We didn't cheat."

Maddie didn't believe her. But even if she did...

"You had an emotional affair with my fiancé." She gritted the words out and Kayla had the grace to blush.

"It's not about Cody," Maddie continued. "It's about trust."

Kayla had no answer to that.

Maddie turned and headed to the door, stopping when Kayla said her name only because there was a crowd outside and she didn't want to push her way through.

"Maddie, give yourself some time to cool off. This isn't the time to make decisions like this."

Maddie whirled around, opened her mouth to tell Kayla what she thought of her suggestion, then abruptly closed it again. Words failed her.

Kayla lifted her chin. "Besides that, you have to give me first refusal on your half of the business. It's in the contract."

"Do you want it?" Maddie asked coldly.

"I do." Kayla's expression was no longer contrite.

"But can you afford it?" It was no secret that Kayla liked to live large, and while the woman was fiscally responsible with the store, she did tend to push the boundaries in her private life. "The contract gives you four weeks to come up with financing."

"I'll look into it," Kayla said before adding on a hopeful note, "unless you would agree to payments for your half?"

And thus prolong their relationship? Not if Maddie could help it. "I want out. If I can find a buyer, I'm selling." Plus, she wanted a lump sum so that she had a cushion while she figured out next moves.

"I get to approve the new buyer," Kayla said flatly. It sounded like a threat.

At the time they'd drawn up the contract, that clause had seemed a good protection. Like Kayla, Maddie had not relished the idea of her partner selling to a stranger. But from the way Kayla was studying her, Maddie wondered if she would approve of anyone, or if she would simply shut Maddie's choices down, thus forcing her to continue ownership, which would translate into being an absentee owner. She'd get a smaller part of the profits because she'd have to hire someone to take her place on the floor. It went without saying that she would *not* smile and make nice with the woman who'd cheated her in more ways than one. Life was too short to put up with that.

For a moment they faced off, then Kayla's expression shifted. "I'm sorry, Maddie. I didn't mean for this to happen. I want to buy you out, but if I can't then you'll have to find someone I can work with. I won't make things difficult. I promise."

"More difficult," Maddie muttered. "I'll be in touch." In the meantime she would endure the weeks of Kayla trying to find financing, followed by the search for a buyer when her partner failed to do that.

She turned and strode to the door. The wedding march played, and Maddie considered it a win that she didn't smash the electric eye with her purse.

SEAN HAD JUST carried the fifth saddle back to the tack shed and picked up the sixth to start cleaning when Maddie drove into the ranch. He thought about ducking into his cabin, but she was going to see his new injury eventually, so it seemed best to get it over with. He brushed snow off the top rail of the pole fence in front of the cabin and set the saddle on it, then headed for the truck with his lopsided gait.

"Need help carrying anything?" He looked past her into the surprisingly empty back seat. If she'd gone to the store, she hadn't spent much time there. He shot Maddie a look, found her gaze riveted onto his black-and-blue cheek.

"What happened to you?"

"An exercise in problem solving."

Maddie gave him a skeptical look. "What happened?"

His don't-talk-about-it mechanism kicked into gear, but he managed to stop it before it came up to speed. The reason he'd met her at the truck was to get explanations out of the way. "I got locked in the stock trailer by a freak blast of wind, managed to get myself out, then fell on the ice."

Maddie put a hand to her lips. "So you

conquered the trailer, then the universe smacked you down?"

"That pretty much sums it up."

He lightly touched the side of his face, glad that the skin was only bruised and not broken, but he might be looking at a black eye. "The embarrassing part is that I felt so victorious before I hit the ice." He usually didn't volunteer stuff like that, but Maddie would appreciate the irony.

"Pride goeth before the fall?"

"Literally. How was your trip to town? Any adventures?"

He spoke wryly, not intending to cause color to rise in Maddie's cheeks, but it did. For a moment he thought she wasn't going to answer, then she said, "I ran into Cody."

He waited.

Maddie shrugged. "It's going to happen in a small town."

"So you're good?"

She wasn't. Was she still carrying a torch for the guy? Sean didn't think so, but the thought made his stomach tighten in an uncomfortable way.

"I'm good," she said lightly. "With practice, it's going to get easier." She glanced over her shoulder at the lodge. "I have a few things to attend to. I'll see you later." She gave him a faint smile. "Feel better."

She turned and headed to the lodge.

Sean tipped back his hat as he watched her go. Definitely not okay. He hated feeling helpless, but this was her battle and unless she asked for help—and there wasn't much he could do about her and Cody living in the same area—there was nothing he could do.

CHAPTER THIRTEEN

"I THINK THERE'S something bugging Maddie." Dillon spoke from the interior of the engine compartment, his voice muffled, but not so much that Sean couldn't make out what he'd said.

After the successful radiator transplant, the kid had asked for help chasing down an electrical issue that affected his rear turn signal. Sean had kind of hoped the kid would tell him what was on his mind, but instead he spoke of Maddie.

"What makes you say that?"

"You need to see for yourself. She's..." Dillon made a circular gesture with one hand.

"Like that?"

Dillon gave a deep nod.

"Did you talk to her?"

"No," Dillon said as if the thought was too scary to contemplate. "I saw her through the kitchen window. She was cutting out cookies like she was about to murder someone with the cookie cutter."

"A case of aggressive baking?"

"My experience there is limited."

Sean would have smiled if a gut-level sense of protectiveness hadn't started poking at him. Maddie had gone to town, came home empty-handed, and now she was murdering cookie dough.

"She saw Cody today."

"Oh." Dillon blew out a breath. "Sucks." He made a scoffing noise. "At least this time it isn't my fault."

"It never was," Sean said, inspecting the harness of wires at the side of the engine block. Everything seemed intact, but he had a feeling that Dillon's electrical problem stemmed from rodents eating the plastic casing over the wiring somewhere in the truck's interior.

They continued to follow the wires until Dillon made a triumphant noise. "I found it."

Sean took a look, then nodded. The plastic had been chewed and the bare wire was touching the engine block. "We can take care of this with tape."

"Duct?"

"Electrical."

Dillon taped up the wire using the proper tape, thus insulating it from surrounding metal, then tested the light. It worked.

"This is therapeutic," Dillon said as he closed the hood. "Maybe I should rethink my teaching plans."

"Just...do something you like."

"Like you did rodeo?"

"Yeah, but don't do it to the detriment of other things."

"Meaning?"

Sean shook his head, and Dillon didn't press. Instead he said, "Maybe you can check on Maddie. Make sure she's like, okay?"

"Yeah. Might be a good idea."

When Sean walked into the lodge kitchen fifteen minutes later, Maddie wasn't assaulting cookie dough, but when she looked up at him, Sean could see why Dillon was concerned. Her face was pale. She didn't have the look of someone who'd been crying. Instead she looked like someone who needed to cry, but couldn't kick the mechanism into gear.

He stopped a good ten feet away from her, giving her space, waiting for her cue.

The cue came fast and hard. Maddie swallowed, then crossed the distance between them and wrapped her arms around his waist, leaning into him.

He smoothed his hands over her back, then held her, the underside of his chin resting on top of her silky head. She didn't cry, but her breathing was uneven, as if she couldn't get it together well enough to cry. She shuddered and moved to push her forehead against his chest. If her eyes were open, she'd be staring at their boots.

When he finally eased back far enough to tip her chin up so that he could see her face, her eyes were closed and unshed tears clung to her lashes.

"Hey," he said, wishing he had a more expansive comfort vocabulary. He didn't. He frankly sucked at comfort...but he wanted things to be different with Maddie. And Dillon, for that matter. His tiny wannabe family.

Temporary wannabe family.

"I hate to ask."

The words were lame, but appeared to be exactly what Maddie needed. She pulled in a breath that made her body shake, and then eased back far enough to see him, keeping her hands on his forearms.

"Cody and Kayla," she said. "My business partner and my fiancé are…" She didn't finish. Didn't need to.

Sean's fingers tightened on her waist. "How do you know this?"

"Oh. I happened to catch them when I stopped by the shop to find out what was going on in my place of business. They were in the break room. Now I know why they didn't want me to go into the vault. There was no cat in there—just a cheating ex-fiancé."

Sean uttered a low curse.

"I asked how long it had been going on. Kayla said two weeks. Cody said since Labor Day. My business partner lied to me. The person I trust with the books, with *ev-*

erything, lied to me. To. My. Face. At least Cody was honest. Now." Her voice rang with bitterness. "How can I work with her?" she asked. "How can I—"

She broke off abruptly and pulled away, hugging her arms to her middle, but she did not cry. Sean sensed how important it was for her not to.

It took most of his mental resolve to keep from reaching out to her, gathering her tightly against him and protecting her from the hurt.

As much as he wanted to, he couldn't shield her, but he could…what? Confront Cody? It sounded like he was the more honest of the two, but Sean wasn't giving the guy a pass. The guy had been carrying on in Maddie's place of business and that was not cool.

On instinct he reached for her, and Maddie walked back into his arms, her head coming to rest on his shoulder, her body pliant, as if she didn't have the strength to fight off the comfort that he was offering.

So this was how comfort worked: instinct put into action.

He held her until the scent of burning cookies and the smoke alarm could no longer be ignored.

"I'll get those," she said with a little sniff, easing herself out of his embrace.

"Let me." He spoke quietly, and while Maddie didn't articulate an agreement, she didn't stop him.

Once the pan of smokers was out of the oven and Maddie had waved a towel at the smoke alarm until it stopped ringing, they left the pan on the sideboard and Sean gestured toward the hall.

"Come on. I'll pour you a drink."

She shook her head. "No drink. I just need… I don't know…to come to terms with the fact that I can't trust anyone?"

He took her hand and led her to the main hall and sat on the sofa where he'd been sitting when Max and Shirl had explained how the two of them would be working together. It would have been helpful of them to warn him that he might end up on the verge of falling in love with his fellow lodge-keeper if he didn't watch himself, but they hadn't, so there they were.

"Do you mind if I have one?"

Maddie shook her head, focusing on the flames. Sean poured, then settled at the sofa. Maddie curled up beside him, her shoulder almost, but not quite, touching his. He drew in the sweet scent of her shampoo and then slid a hand along the back of the sofa behind her. Still they did not touch.

The fire flickered and Sean sipped his scotch, barely tasting the smoky undertones.

"I told Kayla I'm selling my half," Maddie said. "I have to find a buyer she agrees to."

"Can you sell to her?"

"She wants my half, but I don't think she can swing it."

"There's got to be a way. Business loans. Things like that." He had no idea what he was talking about, but surely there were options.

"Kayla is a big fan of revolving credit, and I don't have high hopes of her getting a loan. She has four weeks to find financing. If she fails, I find a buyer. She approves and I go on my way. The only thing is…after that I have to come up with my next act."

"Any ideas?" he asked softly, allowing his fingertips to brush her shoulder. He knew this "what next?" feeling well.

"Well," she said ironically, "I could go to work for a bakery. You saw how good I was with the cookies tonight."

Sean let his arm settle around her shoulders and she snuggled into him. "I don't know. I have a degree in business. I'll be able to find something. I just won't be my own boss."

She sighed and let her head rest against his shoulder. "What if I can't find a buyer? The longer I'm tied to that woman…" She let out a low growl.

"Take it easy," Sean said softly. "Things will—"

"Work out?" she asked with a wry lift of her eyebrows.

Sean felt the smack of irony, but he did not flinch. "Maybe so."

"I'll have to hire someone to take my place. I will not work with someone I don't trust and Kayla is now number one on that list. I'll also have to address my living arrangements because, you know what? I'm here on the Lucky Creek Ranch *temporarily.*"

Sean understood her concern. If she paid to have someone work for her, that would chisel away at a housing budget and unless she wanted to take advantage of Max's charity, she had to find an affordable place to live. "You know," he said slowly. "I'll loan you the—"

Her fierce expression had the remaining words dying on his lips.

"No," she said simply. "You will not. I can handle this."

"Alone?"

"Just like you. Yes."

THE CHRISTMAS PARADE and the open house were a day away, and Maddie had thankfully been able to bury herself in prep work. Holly was catering, but Maddie decided that there was no reason she couldn't add to the festivities by doing some of her own baking, only this time she wasn't allowing her cookies to light on fire.

Dillon pitched in to help and it was during their baking time that Maddie discovered why he'd been so distracted…he'd fallen for the wrestling coach's daughter.

"Does she know?" Maddie asked as she rolled dough.

"I don't know. She might suspect."

Maddie let out a mental sigh as she did a flashback to high school days. "Do you think she likes you?"

"Maybe, but I can't do anything because it's a conflict of interest." Maddie made a confused face and he said, "She's my coach's daughter?"

That seemed like an easy fix. "Ask her out when the season is over."

"That's all well and good, but Rod Ellis also likes her, and he plays basketball. No conflict."

"Ask her to wait for you?"

Dillon rolled his eyes and then attacked the dough with a cookie cutter using quick choppy motions.

"Easy. You'll cut through the mat."

He gave her a look she didn't understand, then settled into a gentler rhythm of cutting. Maddie, having exhausted her supply of helpful suggestions for unrequited love, slid a sheet of cookies into the oven and set the timer.

"I don't want to say anything until after the season ends and, in the meantime, Rod Ellis is going to slither in and talk Taylor into going out with him."

"Talk to her. Explain conflict of interest."

"Big risk."

"Yeah. I know." Maddie started rolling dough on her side of the marble counter. "That's what life is all about, I guess."

"I'll figure something out," he muttered. "It's just kind of hard to hang everything out there, and possibly be obliterated."

She knew about that.

"Speaking of hanging it out there," Dillon said, "do you think Sean is nervous about the parade?"

"Probably."

"At least his face isn't purple on the side where he fell anymore. More yellow now. Mitch will appreciate that."

Maddie couldn't help laughing. Dillon looked up at her and then grinned. "Sean doesn't believe that people want to see him."

"I know."

"Do you think he's shy or just generally grumpy," he asked.

"Grumpy. For sure."

Dillon laughed as he pushed the cookie cutter into the dough and Maddie smiled to herself, surprised that she couldn't remember the last time he'd been grumpy with her.

As Mitch promised, the Western Santa costume fit. Thankfully, Sean could supply most of it himself—jeans, black belt with a big shiny rodeo buckle, black hat. The mercantile provided a red-and-black buffalo plaid shirt, a holly green wild rag, a long brown duster coat and a fake beard. Sean did not want to think about how many people had worn and breathed into the beard ahead of him. He was just happy he didn't have to wear velvet and fur.

"Most people wear the mustache under their chin," the man who'd given him the costume to try on said. "But maybe you should go full face," he added, taking in the yellow and violet remnants of the bruise on

Sean's face. The guy sucked air from between his teeth and said, "If you don't mind me asking, what happened?"

"I fell down," Sean said.

Obviously disappointed that he hadn't done hand-to-hand combat with a wild bronc or bull, the man said, "We're really glad you agreed to do this. We used to have our own local celebrity cowboy here—Ross Callahan, the roper. Do you know him?"

"He's pretty famous," Sean said. To the point that Sean didn't feel qualified to fill his shoes—or suit or whatever. Ross Callahan had been reigning world champion tie down roper when Sean was a teen, and he didn't relinquish the crown for a long, long time.

"He wore this stuff?" Sean asked.

"Until he outgrew it. This was the original outfit from about twenty years ago. I got it out because I thought it would fit you better."

Not only did it fit, but it was also in good shape considering its age. Sean would have loved to own the classic shearling lined drover coat, which was much better than his own.

"Ross had to go into assisted care last year and we didn't have a grand marshal, which was a real disappointment to the folks. Then we lined up Willie Marx for this year."

Sean's eyebrows lifted. Marx was a well-known bull rider from the northeastern corner of the state.

"Yeah," the man continued, "he got creamed in his final rodeo in November. He's in traction. So…we're really glad that you're here. People love a champion."

Sean felt oddly self-conscious. "Yeah. Well…thanks."

"Not that you're third choice or anything," the man said.

"Wouldn't matter if I were," Sean said as he unbuttoned the shirt and handed it over along with the wild rag and duster.

"You can pick these up the morning of the parade. It stages behind the store, so it'll be easy."

"Do I need to come up with candy or anything?"

"Nope. Provided."

"And there's no lap sitting?" He didn't think there was, but he wouldn't put it past Mitch to spring it on him.

"That's for regular Santa, following the parade, in the community hall. Then late afternoon at dusk, families start traveling around to see the lights, and there are a few places that are set as hors d'oeuvre stops—" The guy's eyebrows went up. "I guess you know about that. You're one of them."

"We are," Sean agreed.

"We're really glad that the Tidwells were able to participate this year despite the new schedule. The lodge is the coup de grâce of the tour."

Sean had never been part of a coup de grâce. He thought Maddie would get a kick out of it when he told her. Or rather, she might have before she'd discovered that her business partner was a snake. It killed him watching her work through the BS that her ex and her partner had rained down upon her, but there was nothing he could do except to watch.

After the costume try-on, he headed to the bank with the intention of wiring his funds to MDMI. The day was warm for December, the sky a bright blue, the color of his lucky riding shirt. People seemed to be in two frames of mind as they walked past—preoccupied, moving with their heads down on their way to wherever, or relaxed, strolling instead of walking, peering into store windows and smiling at their neighbors. He was somewhere in between, strolling, but preoccupied—until he was snatched back to reality by the site of one Cody Marsing leaving Maddie's shop by the front door.

No more skulking, it seemed.

Sean slowed his steps, glad to see the man turned in the opposite direction so that he didn't have to debate about punching him out. Actually, he wasn't going to confront the guy. It appeared that Cody was glad to let Maddie be. But...

But.

He walked to the front of the store and stood for a moment, studying the display in the window—a winter bride with a satin fur-trimmed hood and cape. Maddie would have been a winter bride.

He ignored the small part of him that celebrated the fact that she was not and pushed open the door to the store. The wedding march sounded as he walked inside, his boots loud on the hardwood floor. A red-haired woman appeared from the back, all smiles. Was this Maddie's partner?

"Kayla?" he asked, glad that he remembered the woman's name.

"No." Red smiled. "I'll get her."

"Thanks." While he waited, he took in the decor, a mix of Western frou-frou stuff and bridal everything. He lifted the edge of a veil attached to a silver concho barrette and decorated with tiny, embroidered horses. Clever.

"Can I help you?"

"Yeah." Now that he was there, with the woman who was, purposefully or not, making Maddie's life a misery, he knew that he was going to follow through with the crazy plan he'd been toying with since early that morning. "Can we talk in private? It's a financial matter."

"Is this about a dress deposit?"

"This is about me becoming a silent partner in your business."

The alarm on her features told Sean that he'd come at this too abruptly.

"It's not a shakedown," he said quickly. "Maddie Kincaid is a friend of mine. She wants out and rather than wait to find a buyer, I thought that I could, well, finance the buyout."

Kayla still didn't follow him, so he spelled it out slowly.

"I will loan you the money to buy her out. I know what she wants for her half." Kayla tilted her head warily, and Sean gave her the figure that Maddie had tossed out the other night.

"Who are you?" Her gaze traveled over his scarred face as if trying to place him. He knew the moment that she did. "Rodeo Denim Jeans. High Country Whiskey."

He nodded. "Don't forget Crystal Creek Coffee." A short contract, but lucrative.

She tilted her head. He could see that she was not unhappy with the idea of no longer dealing with Maddie or finding a business partner she agreed to.

"And I would then have sole owner-ship—"

"As soon as you pay me back. There are two conditions, though."

She let out a breath, her expression clearly stating that this had obviously been too good to be true.

"Which are?"

"You pay me back in twelve months' time." He would need the money to go to school, which he was going to postpone for a year. "And you don't tell Maddie where the money comes from. A kind of NDA, if you will."

She frowned deeply—or tried to. He had a feeling that some kind of injectable beauty treatment was getting in the way—not that he cared. To each their own.

"Why not just give Maddie the money and have her pay you back?"

"Because I don't know that she would say yes." He was certain that she wouldn't.

"What about the contract." Kayla cleared her throat. "If I were to say yes."

"We can use a DIY site online." She gave him a skeptical look and he said, "Your attorney can look it over. There's not much to it." He'd looked into it that morning after growing weary of lying awake wondering if Maddie was also lying awake.

Kayla considered for a moment, studying the floor near her white Western boots. "I don't see how I can pay you back in one year. Two would be more realistic."

Which, in turn, meant that it would be two years until he could pay tuition. But maybe he could take out a loan himself. He'd have a bridal shop for collateral. He'd figure it out later.

"And what about interest?"

He gave her a tight smile. "Interest-free loan for one year. Interest on the second year."

"You must really like her."

"Here's my number." He scrawled his phone number on a floral pad sitting on the glass-top counter. "Talk it over with Cody."

Kayla's mouth opened, then closed again and she nodded.

Sean let himself out of the store to the

cheery wedding march, and stepped onto the sidewalk. He reached for his phone and punched Finn's number as he walked. "Hey," he said. "I suppose the livestock manager job has been filled."

"It was," Finn said.

Sean ran a hand over the side of his face as he bumped up against the inevitable—for now, anyway. "I'm postponing school for a year." Even if Kayla didn't take him up on his offer, or if Maddie said no to the deal, he would miss the deadline to pay tuition. He was okay with that. "How do things look for getting a night calving job in Wyoming?"

Finn let out a choked laugh. "There's always a call for night calvers in Wyoming. But you'll have to start soon. First calves due to drop the first week of January."

"Send me the details." He was going to have to invest in more winter wear if he was going to brave January nights outdoors.

Sean ended the call and headed to his truck. Now all he had to do was wait for Kayla to cut Maddie loose—if Maddie wanted to go, that is. As he saw it, he'd given her an out. If she chose to continue the ownership of her shop, she had the option. If not, she had cash. Either way she won, in a way.

Totally worth the sacrifice.

CHAPTER FOURTEEN

IN YEARS PAST, Maddie and Kayla had stood outside of their shop to watch the Larkspur Christmas parade and then retired inside to serve cookies and warm cider to holiday shoppers. Very few shoppers were interested in purchasing a wedding or prom dress during the holidays, but Kayla and Maddie still went all out in the spirit of community building.

This year Maddie had an entirely different agenda, starting with making certain that Lucky Creek Guest Ranch was ready for open house guests. The photo spread in the paper had been better than either she or Sean had anticipated. Sean, having ticked off the photographer, had his money on a couple of blurry shots, but instead the photo of the main hall of Lucky Creek Ranch had taken up most of the front page of the paper below the fold.

And that meant a lot of guests, Dillon predicted. "They don't stay that long. It's more of a steady stream. But if we can win the token battle, Mom will be pleased."

The token battle being the online voting for the best this and that. Best lights. Best ambiance. Best Santa. And, of course, the a winner.

"It's not that important," Dillon assured them before loading his gym bag in his newly repaired truck, but Maddie had a feeling that the kid really wanted to win. They'd kept themselves busy touching up this and that, until Dillon announced it was time for him to meet his team.

"I'd better go, too," Sean said. He wore new jeans, so dark that Maddie guessed they'd never been washed, polished black cowboy boots, and his regular blue flannel chore shirt.

Maddie tapped his chest. "Not very Santa-like."

"I'm not Santa. Just a cowboy facsimile."

"Are you wearing the beard?"

He rubbed his bruised face, amusement in his eyes. "I was encouraged to do so."

Maddie laughed and Sean grinned back. "I'll pick up the rest of the costume at the mercantile."

He explained that the shirt, wild rag and duster he'd be borrowing had been worn by a rodeo luminary back in the day. Maddie knew that luminary. Ross Callahan had taught the members of her 4-H club to throw a loop when she was twelve, but she'd been more interested in speed, and had committed to barrel racing instead of roping.

"I'm surprised the outfit fits," she said. "I remember Ross being kind of...round?"

"But once upon a time he was more elongated. I'm wearing *that* outfit."

Maddie laughed again, a nice change from ruminating about things out of her control for too many hours. She'd finally concluded in the early morning hours that she was going to have to bend a little to make this situation work. Instead of instantly putting out feelers for a buyer, she would wait to see if Kayla could find financing. It was possible...but Maddie wasn't holding her breath.

Maybe she *would* end up financing her ex-partner's buyout, as much as she didn't want to for both fiscal and personal reasons. She might even return to work rather than pay someone to take her place. *Maybe.* It would be awkward, but more cost-effective.

And it might make Kayla really uncomfortable.

Maddie didn't try to shush her small voice, uncharitable as it was.

She arrived in Larkspur an hour before the parade was to begin, and as Dillon had promised, found a parking spot behind the main street businesses in the staging area at the end of town.

It wasn't difficult to find Sean, who was already on the lead float, ready to perform his grand marshal duties which included smiling, waving and nodding. Heavy stuff for a guy who only liked being looked at when he was bronc riding. But at least he had a beard to hide behind.

Regardless of what he'd told her, he was the only Santa in the parade, and, in Maddie's book, that made him the Santa—at least until lap-sitting Santa showed up at the community center. Sean Arteaga as Santa. What was the world coming to?

She saw no reason to touch base with him, but he caught sight of her and waved her over before she slipped away, and his obvious relief at seeing her made that warm heady feeling she now associated with the guy take over.

"Looking good," she said as she approached. "At least you have a chair. For a couple of years they perched Ross on this fake horse they retired from the roof of the Western store."

"I'm ready for this to be over."

A teen wearing a Larkspur Larks letter jacket jogged up carrying a giant bag of candy. "This is in case you run out. Micky will keep your basket filled."

Micky, a skinny boy in a cowboy elf costume nodded vigorously. Sean thanked both and then met Maddie's eyes. She read so many things in their blue depths, "save me" being the clearest message there.

She reached out to take his hand. He

squeezed her fingers and smiled, albeit weakly.

"You're a big bad bronc rider. You've got this."

His eyebrows drew together in a serious expression. "I am kind of big and bad, aren't I?"

"The baddest." She took a backward step. "I'm going to find a place to watch where I don't have to see Kayla standing in front of our store."

Sean nodded, his expression shifting behind the beard. "I'll meet you after?"

She shook her head. "I'll be headed straight back to the ranch so that I'm there in time to plug everything in."

"I might pass you on the road."

She squeezed his fingers and let go. "Break a leg." One corner of her mouth quirked. "Maybe that's not appropriate for parades."

"It's fine for parades. Not for rodeos." He patted his bad leg. "Too suggestive of reality."

Maddie found a spot to watch the parade a block up from Spurs and Veils, on the same side of the street, which meant that her gaze wouldn't accidentally wander toward her store.

She was going to have to grow more of a spine by mid-January, but for now, she was giving herself a break, allowing a few weenie-outs.

The local kazoo band was tuning up not far from where she stood near the start of the route, her thinking being that she could escape via the back streets as soon as the last float entered Main Street. Soon the high school marching band drowned out the kazoos as they signaled the start of the action.

Maddie leaned against a holly wrapped lamppost, ready for her first solo parade watch in years.

"Mad!"

She frowned, then turned to find Danna Elliot pushing through the crowd, saying "Excuse me" several times as she moved, making her way to Maddie.

"I just want to tell you how much I love the gown you designed for me. Ashley is already at work, using that dress Kayla gave her. Thank you so much!"

"Which design did you choose?"

"That floaty one from the old movie. It's so much less cliché than what I had planned, and it will look great with my custom boots. White with pink and yellow butterflies."

"That sounds amazing," Maddie said. She meant it. Working on the design hadn't been easy, but it had been healing.

"And I'm buying that veil. The one on the barrette."

"That's one of a kind, you know."

"Just like me."

Maddie grinned. That was exactly what she'd told Danna when the girl had been afraid that she was weird at the start of her sixth-grade year in school.

Danna reached out and hugged her tightly. "Thank you. I need to get back to my family." She took a step, then stopped and turned back. "Should I send the invitation to the shop?" Because Maddie was no longer at her regular address on the Marsing Ranch.

"Send it to the Lucky Creek Ranch," Maddie said. "I'll get it there."

Danna waved and Maddie turned to the street as the marching band started playing, "It's Beginning to Look a Lot Like Christmas." A moment later the band appeared, marching four deep. The speaker above Maddie's head announced the names of the band members as they marched by, then came the sports teams, all dressed in different renditions of Christmas costumes.

Next came horses, the kazoo band and several floats from local businesses, all flinging candy.

Apparently, Sean's float hadn't been slated to lead the parade as he'd thought. Maddie was wondering if something had gone wrong, when she felt a tap on her shoulder. She turned and her features tightened as she found Kayla standing behind her.

"I'd like to talk to you after the parade," she said quietly, so quietly that Maddie barely heard her over the kazoos.

"Fine. At the shop?" Maddie asked. Kayla nodded. "Will Cody be there?"

"No."

"Then I'll see you there."

Kayla disappeared back into the crowd, leaving Maddie to watch the rest of the parade without really enjoying it. All she could think was, *What now?* And try as she might to push the thought away and focus on the fun of the day, she couldn't.

The only high point was when the announcer said, "And let's hear it for this year's guest of honor and cowboy Santa, Mr. Sean Arteaga!"

A cheer went up, and Maddie found herself smiling. That had to perk up a big bad bronc rider who didn't like to be looked at. At least he knew he was appreciated. His float came into view, and the cowboy and cowgirl elves started throwing candy to the public. People waved, and Sean waved back. Maddie thought that she might be the only person there who could read his discomfort. He caught sight of her, and she thought he probably flashed her a grin from behind the beard because his eyes crinkled.

"What happened to your face?" a little boy yelled out not far from her. His mother shushed him, but Sean had heard.

"I slipped," he called. "Keep hold of your mom's hand when you walk on the ice."

The boy looked down at the ground as if checking for ice, then beamed up at Sean as he went by.

Well played, Maddie thought. She waited until the crowd around her started to thin, then decided to face the inevitable and made her way to the shop where Kayla and Elsa were already serving cider and cookies.

Maddie walked through the staging area to the back, where not that long ago she'd discovered the truth about her trusted partner and her trusted former fiancé.

Kayla followed and as soon as the door was closed she folded her arms over her chest and said, "Some options have presented themselves…"

"Options?" Maddie asked after Kayla's voice petered out.

The woman let out a breath and glanced down as if searching for words, then raised her gaze and started over. "I want to buy you out. I have tentative financing if the price is right."

Maddie stared at her business partner for several seconds before reminding herself to breathe. "How?"

It was a legit question, since Kayla tended to keep her credit cards maxed out, and also had a car payment, a mortgage payment and who knew what other kind of payment.

"That isn't important."

And it wasn't Maddie's business.

"What's your offer?" Maddie couldn't help the suspicious note in her voice. If Kayla had financing, it may well be from Cody, although Maddie didn't see how, because he was dealing with financial issues of his own as he worked to build his carpentry business. But did she really care where the money came from?

No.

Kayla lifted her chin and stated an amount less than the price Maddie had thrown out to Sean. It was close to fair since it was mainly inventory and fixtures that she was buying, but still a lowball offer.

"Well?" Kayla finally said.

Maddie silently studied the woman who'd had a hand in turning her life upside down.

Maybe someday she'd be able to face her and not feel a sense of betrayal.

Someday.

In the meantime she wasn't going to accept less than she wanted. Maddie's mouth shifted sideways and then she threw out the number higher than the one she'd told Sean was fair.

She'd expected more haggling, but to her surprise, Kayla nodded.

"Done."

SEAN SURVIVED THE Christmas parade, and he'd even been asked out by an attractive mercantile employee dressed as an elf after he'd turned in the costume. He'd smiled and said that he was off the market, then crossed the much emptier parking lot to his truck, ready to commence phase two of a very long day. Open house would begin in a matter of hours.

The funny thing was that Dillon had been right about the stupid amount of preparation for a few hours' worth of showing off, but the kid was also excited to host. Maybe the absence of the "parental units" as he called them, contributed. Regardless, he met Sean at his truck when he'd pulled into his usual parking spot, and asked him to park behind the barn because the rest of the driveway was for guest parking.

Sean did as he was asked, and was amused to see that Dillon had brought home a wrestling buddy to help guide cars to parking spots.

"Will we be that busy?"

Dillon shook his head. "Brayden wanted to skip his cousin's open house, so he's coming to ours. I gave him a job as an excuse."

"Gotcha."

Sean headed to the main lodge, assuming that he was dressed well enough for a casual evening of people arriving, gawking, eating hors d'oeuvres and enjoying time with their neighbors.

"This is strange," he commented to Maddie a few hours later. When she wasn't welcoming guests, or helping the catering staff of two, she stood with a satisfied smile on her face—possibly something to do with Kayla texting him to say that she was ready to move forward with the loan which was only a little more than what he'd told her he would lend. He'd agreed to the new number.

"What's strange," she asked.

"People coming and going. Enjoying themselves with no particular goal in mind—"

"Other than enjoying themselves?"

"Yeah. I might have to try this sometime. Usually I just hide out during the holidays." Losing his parents had a lot to do with that, as did not being super close to anyone in recent years, other than Finn and a few assorted rodeo buddies. Once Shay left, he'd cocooned.

"I spent mine with Cody's family for the past three years. I'm glad I have something different to do this year."

"You don't want to spend the holidays with Cody's family?" he asked innocently.

She gave him a scowling look, then took his chin in her hand and kissed him soundly for the second time that evening. He'd attributed the first kiss, which happened just before the guests stared arriving, to nerves. He glanced down at Maddie as she resumed her place beside him, innocently scanning the room. She didn't look nervous.

"I'll take that as a no?" he said.

She nudged his side without looking at him, and he was aware of just how much he was coming to care for this woman... whom he was lying to by omission.

For her peace of mind. It isn't like she's being forced into the sale.

Kayla's offer gave her a choice as to whether or not to get out of an uncomfortable situation. The only thing she didn't know and didn't need to know was where Kayla had gotten the loan.

The results counterbalanced the subterfuge.

No matter what she chose to do, he would be attending the diesel institute a year from now. He'd already alerted the school that he'd encountered an unforeseen circumstance and was now slated to attend next January. He had enough money left in his nest egg to see him through a couple of lean months, and to pay Finn, who had nailed down the night calver job for him.

He'd spoken to Max that morning, explaining that he had a paying job lined up and offering to find a replacement come January, even though Maddie had insisted she needed no help. Max had assured him that there was no need. Dillon and Maddie could handle the chores now that Sean had all the waterers up and running with new heaters.

He was, in other words, superfluous on the Lucky Creek, just as Dillon had said.

It wasn't a good feeling, but it allowed him to leave. He needed to leave, both for financial reasons and to sort out his feelings for one Maddie Kincaid. All he'd asked of Max was to allow him to tell Dillon and Maddie.

"Penny for your thoughts," Maddie murmured.

"I'm not falling for *that* again," he muttered back.

He felt her shoulders shake with silent laughter before her body went still. Then she pushed off the table where they'd been leaning side by side and crossed to greet the women who'd just come in the door—close friends, he gathered, from the way they hugged and laughed and hugged again. She waved him over and was introduced to her Best. Friends. Ever! Whitney Fox and Kat Farley. Also with them was a cowboy he did recognize, Troy Mackay, who held a baby girl in one arm. She waved a chubby fist at Sean and gave him a drippy smile.

"Good to see you." Troy held out his free hand, which Sean took. "Sorry to hear about your wreck."

Sean knew that Troy had had wrecks of his own, so he merely shrugged and then Maddie came to his side, leaning into him as if to claim him while she chatted with her friends, and he continued discussing rodeo wrecks with Troy whom he gathered was in a relationship with Kat.

At one point when Troy was attending to something Kat had asked, and Maddie was talking to Whitney with her arm pressed firmly against his, Sean realized that he liked this feeling of belonging way too much.

Best not get used to it.

He acknowledged the truth of those words, albeit grudgingly. Someday, when he wasn't in a state of flux, brought about by his own poor planning, he'd seek out a place where he belonged, maybe even with Maddie, although he was afraid of jinxing that by considering it too hard.

This was not the time, when he was about to head south to spend a few frigid months keeping calves from freezing to death after birth.

Maddie returned to hostess duties in short order, and her friends left not long after with a promise to get together early the following week. Sean saw them out, and was rewarded by a speculative look along with a "see you later" from Whitney Fox.

He was pretty sure Whitney had guessed that he wasn't immune to Maddie, but he and Maddie had acted like a couple, so what did he expect? It wasn't like he could run after her and explain that he was a rebound guy.

If Whitney was as close of a friend as she seemed, then, yeah. She already knew.

"WASN'T IT GREAT?" Dillon said. "I told you it would be great. We're going to win the token battle for sure."

His friend Brayden nodded enthusiastically. "This place always has the best decorations."

"Darned straight," Dillon said.

Sean shot a look at Maddie and there was something about the softness in her expression as she met his gaze that made his breath hitch. There'd been a lot of casual touching that evening, and she'd kissed him.

It all felt very...

Don't say it.

Right. It felt right, but it was an illusion. The open house had been a rousing success—Dillon had already sent his parents updates and videos—and everyone was feeling flush with victory and relieved that it was finally over, and they could settle back into real life.

Where he was superfluous.

He didn't take that seriously because he'd been useful around the place, but Max was right that unless Dillon hit a tree, or the waterers froze, he really wasn't needed. Maddie could drive a tractor and feed the cattle, as could Dillon. Two people could handle the scaled down responsibilities of a guest ranch. There were only supposed to be two of them in the first place. Then Maddie had her life crisis and there were three.

And who knew? Maybe Maddie would stay on at the Lucky Creek in a management role or something after getting out from under the shop.

A screech of chair legs on the tile brought him out of his thoughts.

Dillon and Brayden were on their feet. "I need to get a room ready for Bray," Dillon said. "One of the benefits of living in a guest lodge is that you're set up for guests."

They disappeared down the hall, Brayden laughing at an impression Dillon made of one of their wrestling buddies.

"And here we are," Maddie said. She reached across the table and took Sean's hands. "I have news."

"Yeah?"

"Kayla might be able to buy the shop."

She spoke softly and Sean managed a look of fleeting surprise.

"I know," she said as he set his free hand on top of hers. "I didn't think that was an option." She shrugged, the quiet look of satisfaction that played over her pretty features making Sean wish he didn't have to ruin the moment.

"I have news, too," he said solemnly. "I took a job night calving."

"What?"

"Hear me out. I decided to put off school for a year."

"Why?"

"I'm not ready yet. I'll get more out of it if I wait until next year."

Maddie pulled her hand out from under his. "Really?" She spoke flatly. "I know how this works."

"How?" He didn't know what she was getting at.

"You'll find a reason to put it off next year, too."

"I won't."

"You are now."

"Is it important to you that I go to school?"

She reached out to take loose hold of the front of his shirt. "It's important to me that you get the life that you deserve. You deserve a steady career, not some temp job freezing your butt off."

"Yet," he said quietly, as her hand fell away. "It's my decision to make."

She drew in a breath, opened her mouth, then exhaled slowly instead of speaking. Finally she said, "I can't argue with that."

Sean cocked his head at her. "How would you feel about me if I were only a ranch hand?"

"About you as a person? The same as I feel now. About your future? Worried. Ranch owners come and go, and so do ranch hands at the whim of the owner."

"Ms. Kincaid." The caterer who'd been busy packing up dishes called from the kitchen. "We're finished cleaning. We just need to haul some things to the van and we're done."

Maddie rose to her feet and crossed to the hall leading to the kitchen, where she stood talking to the caterer. Sean also pushed his chair back, intent on making his escape while he could.

He was about to grab his coat from the

back of the leather sofa where he'd laid it earlier, when Maddie said, "Stop."

He did, turning a curious gaze her way. The expression on her face as she crossed the room toward him told the tale. She was starting to piece things together—in a serious way, judging from the sudden intensity of her gaze.

"Did you...?" She shook her head. "No." But she meant yes. "Sean?"

She'd nailed him, so he confessed.

"I loaned Kayla the money to buy you out."

For a long moment Maddie simply stared at him, a look of betrayal twisting her delicate features. "Did she ask you?"

He gave his head a grim shake. "I offered."

"Without telling me."

"You would have said no." *And you needed the option to get out.*

"Undo the offer."

"Can't."

"Have papers been signed?"

"Close to it."

"This is why you aren't going to your diesel class."

He shifted his weight, but didn't answer.

"I'm not going to be part of this deal."

"You may as well, Maddie. I can't use the money this year. One of us may as well get some use out of it."

"You don't get it," she said. She swallowed as she turned her back, then walked toward the fireplace where the pine logs snapped and crackled, cheerfully mocking the tension between them. "It's not the money, Sean. It's trust."

"Did you trust me not to loan Kayla money?"

"No. I trusted you to be open with me about things that affect me."

"Can you look me in the eye and tell me that you wouldn't have said no?" She could not, and she let her silence answer for her. "I wanted to do this," he continued. "It was important to me to help you get out from under this situation."

"Why?"

He drew in a long breath before turning to face the woman who'd come to mean everything to him. "It seemed the only option to help. I messed up by not telling you, but you know what? I'd probably do it again if it helped you out of a bind."

Maddie's lips were pressed tightly together as if she was afraid of what she might say. She turned, facing the fire. The muted noise of the caterers taking their leave suddenly seemed louder than before.

"Maddie..." He followed her, put a gentle hand on her shoulder. Her muscles stiffened at his touch, and he let his hand fall away.

"You need to go." She spoke to the fire, her voice barely more than a whisper.

Sean didn't argue, but it took everything he had to force himself to move. Maddie continued to stare at the fire as he shrugged into the coat, then set his hat on his head. He opened the door and stepped out into the frigid night. Nothing. He closed the door then set off down the flagstone walk to the gate, striding past lights and the reindeer and the sleigh. He crossed the distance to his cabin, barely aware of the ache in his leg.

They would talk later. And he would get Maddie to see that while he should have cleared things with her first—even though that would have been impossible because she would *not* have allowed him to do what he'd done—his solution worked for both of them. He was simply putting his plans on hold, not abandoning them.

Surely, after having time to consider the situation, Maddie would understand.

KAYLA WASN'T ANSWERING her phone—or she specifically wasn't answering Maddie's calls.

How was Maddie supposed to cancel a deal if the other party wouldn't take her calls?

Maybe she wasn't taking any calls. Kayla and Cody were probably out on the town, celebrating the fact that Kayla was about to be the sole owner of Spurs and Veils.

Or so she thought.

Maddie had other ideas. She dropped the phone beside her on the bed where she lay fully dressed. The caterers were gone, Dillon and his friend were in their rooms, and she assumed that Sean was in his cabin, which left her sharing a space with her rampaging thoughts and emotions.

How could he do this? Breach her trust by manipulating things behind her back?

He thought he was doing a good thing, her small voice whispered.

And that's a problem, her stronger inner voice retorted. A big, big problem. Maddie pulled a pillow over her eyes, shutting out the twinkling lights that showed through her window, and stared into nothingness.

Good intentions didn't take away from the fact that Sean had acted without her consent. His argument that she wouldn't have given her consent was totally correct, and he'd overstepped. She wasn't having it.

Yeah? What are you going to do about it?

Face reality. She'd believed that Sean was someone she could trust in a world where secrets kept popping up like mushrooms on an overwatered lawn. But he'd had secrets, too. Secrets that involved her. He'd gone behind her back, left her out of an equation in which her happiness was the result of solving for X.

Suddenly restless, she got out of bed—she never was one for lying about feeling sorry for herself—and walked to the window, where she stared out at the lights, the sleigh, the full moon shining above the tree line, bathing the field in silver light. The cows were lying so close together that it was difficult to distinguish one from another. Simply a black mass huddled close for warmth and security on a winter night.

Maddie turned away from the window, hugged herself.

Tomorrow she would talk to Sean, do a better job of explaining herself after the shock of what he'd done had diminished. He was willing to give up a year of his life for her. That was amazing, but the bottom line was that she hated being the recipient of such a sacrifice and she was going to turn it around. The man was going to school, even if she had to yoke herself to Kayla for the next several years.

She pressed a hand to her forehead as tears stung the corners of her eyes. She blinked them back, focused on the multi-colored twinkling lights, momentarily re-living the fun, the flirting, the kisses that were part of the holiday display.

Things would never be the same between her and Sean.

The realization ruined her.

It also gave her an incentive to look at things differently...to see what, if anything, could be salvaged.

DILLON HAD WARNED Sean that the day after the open house was a letdown, and Sean was indeed feeling low, but it had nothing to do with the big holiday event being behind them. Nope. It had to do with doing the right thing—in his eyes, not Maddie's—and the fallout that ensued.

What he wouldn't give for some mindless tinsel slinging or newel post garland wrapping to take his mind off the problem that loomed before him, that problem being the realization that Maddie was right.

The moon was just dipping below the tree line when Sean got out of bed, and it cast a few silvery rays through the branches as it disappeared from sight. He glanced at the stove clock, then pushed a hand over the top of his head. Four o'clock and nothing to do until daylight, four hours away.

Nothing to do but make coffee and reflect on what he could have done differently in the Maddie situation.

He'd screwed up, but while Maddie was angry with him, she was also now in a position to start a new life without her lying business partner.

Had he gone about it in the right way? Hindsight told him no. That said, Maddie's reaction told him that there would have been no other way to get her to accept the financial bailout than to present it to her as a done deal.

But had that been his call to make?

No matter how he twisted things in his head, he had to admit that if the tables were turned, he'd be ticked off. He could give, but he was a rotten receiver. Maddie was the same.

That left him with two questions: Could he fix matters? Should he try?

And as he ruminated a third question

came to him: Would Maddie be better off without him?

She isn't with you.

He was a rebound guy, and this was the perfect opportunity to leave without hurting Maddie any more than he'd already done. Maybe he'd save himself some pain, too.

Too late.

The truth sucked. Logically he'd always known that they were too different; that it was crazy to think that they might get together at some point in the distant future, after Maddie had gotten over her breakup and he'd nailed down a future.

So now you move on.

He leaned his hands on the sink and stared out the window in the direction of the dark fields as the coffee machine gurgled and spit behind him. He'd let this taste of pretend family life get to him, to make him want things he was not destined to have. It was fun. It was temporary. And now he'd blown it. Not with the money, but with the secrecy. His motives were good, but his execution sucked.

His ruminations were interrupted by

the low vibration of his phone on the bedside table. He crossed the dark room to see who was texting at a ridiculous hour. Finn, with more information about the job he'd agreed to take after a fairly brief phone interview the day before. His rodeo fame, such as it was, got him both the interview and an immediate job offer. The rancher had no issues with Sean's bum leg as long as Sean could handle himself, which Sean was determined to do. It might be good for his leg to get a bit of a workout, built up muscles and all that. He'd be in better shape when he went to school in a year, have more stamina. A gap year, as the kids called it, could be a good thing.

After he'd fired off a Thanks to Finn, along with a question as to whether the guy ever slept, the second message came in.

Do you want to start early? They just lost a guy.

How early?

Finn took his time with the reply, possibly having fallen back asleep, given the hour, then just as Sean set the phone down, it buzzed again.

The day after Christmas.

Probably not. I have commitments.

Did he really? Or did he want a few more days of pretend family, even if part of that pretend family was pissed at him?

The phone buzzed with Finn's reply.

January 2 it is. I'll pass that along.

He carried the phone to the table, in case Finn had more to say, but it remained silent as he drank his coffee, glad for the stillness of the dark morning. Glad for the time to commit to reality now that he wasn't influenced by sparkly lights and holiday cheer and a woman who had gotten under his skin in a very serious way.

Nothing had changed, other than him having bailed out Maddie. He was always going to leave, after all.

And there you have it.

He'd always intended to leave...but his

intentions had gotten muddled as he'd got sucked into Dillon's "we're a team" dynamic. Had he thought that these good times and good feelings were going to last forever?

Of course not. That would be naive, and he was anything but.

He pushed his chair back and was heading toward the shower when a movement outside the window caught his eye. He turned and walked around the kitchen table and pushed the curtain all the way to one side. A cow lumbered past his cabin.

Of course she did. What was a ranch-sitting job without some renegade cow action?

With a shake of his head, he climbed into his winter chore clothing and let himself out of the cabin, spotting first one dark shape in the early morning twilight, then another, and another. A gate banged in the wind, and he crossed the wide driveway to inspect the latch. It was fine. Either the gate hadn't been fastened correctly, or he had a Houdini cow. Either way, he needed to get the girls back into the pasture and there was one surefire way to get the job done before they found the haystack.

"ARE YOU AWAKE?"

Dillon's voice came through Maddie's door not long after she'd finally fallen asleep. She reached for the lamp switch. The last time she'd looked at the clock, it had been 3 a.m. Now it was five.

"Dillon? What's up?"

The moment the question left her lips she heard the sound of an engine not far from her bedroom window.

"Yeah. I don't know what's up, but don't we usually feed the cows after daylight?"

The teen yawned on the last word, but Maddie felt a surge of adrenaline. Why was Sean on the tractor at this hour? A few possibilities shot into her head, and she found that she didn't like any of them. The man was not leaving this ranch until they straightened a few things out—like what he could do with the money he lent Kayla.

"I'll go see what the deal is," she said as she reached for her jeans. "Why don't you head back to bed?"

"As if."

Maddie let out a sigh, but before she could say that she kind of wanted to talk to Sean alone, he said, "Unless I'd be a third wheel."

"You would."

"In that case, I'll see you at ten. Bray should be up by then." He started out of the room, then stopped and turned back. "Unless there's an emergency, that is."

"I'll text you if we need you."

"Okay." Dillon's footsteps receded down the hall and Maddie started pulling on layers of clothing. After dressing, she pulled her hair back in an elastic band and then headed down the dark hallway, through the main hall to the room off the kitchen where she kept her chore coat, hat and boots. By the time she'd started down the flagstone walk, her breath crystallizing in front of her, the lights from the tractor shone in the field. She could see that Sean was hauling a bale of hay and that the cows were following him, but why now?

Was he honestly thinking of leaving today?

She hurried her steps, without pausing to

think why. By the time she reached the gate, which was open, the tractor was within a few yards of it. He drove through and she closed the gate and dropped the latch into place.

"Better do the chain, too," he said after turning off the engine and climbing down out of the cab.

"The cows escaped?"

"But an easy fix." He gestured to the tractor parked near the haystack. "They followed food like a teenage athlete."

Maddie felt the pull of amusement, but she couldn't smile. Neither did he. They stood for a silent moment in the crisp early morning air, a good three feet of trampled snow separating them. Behind Sean the sky was beginning to lighten. It was going to be a beautiful day.

Maybe.

"Are you leaving?" She asked the question that she felt like she didn't have a right to ask, after what had gone down between them the night before.

"I think I should head south and set myself up before starting the job." He toed the snow in front of him. "I won't leave you high and dry—" he held up a hand when Maddie started to speak "—and I'm well aware that you and Dillon can handle the chores." He paused then said, "I'm superfluous, after all."

The wryly spoken words made Maddie draw herself up straighter. "I didn't want you to give up schooling to buy out the shop. That doesn't mean I want you to leave."

"But I need to, Maddie."

"Why?" She wished she hadn't asked because, to her embarrassment, her voice cracked. His expression shifted, softened, and he started to reach for her, then abruptly dropped his hands, as if he'd just remembered that they were no longer on that page.

He gestured at the ranch. "This isn't me. It's not my life. It's been a great vacation from reality, but it's not...what I'm meant for."

She wanted to ask what he was meant for? Pulling calves in freezing temperatures? Putting off school to save a friend... if she was even that. She hadn't allowed herself to think about it, but she was on her way to being something more with him, given time—lots of time—but now he was about to walk away. And she was at a loss as to how to handle it. Had it merely been their different views about him putting off school, she could have come up with an answer, but she sensed it was more than that. It concerned something that she couldn't argue about.

"It's been a vacation from reality for both of us. That doesn't mean—"

"It does," he said solemnly. "You can't build something real with a fantasyland as a base."

"I have no idea what that means." But she did not like the sound of it.

He kicked more snow as he studied his boots. "I'm not good at these kinds of things. I tend to screw up royally."

Again, she didn't know what he meant, but she let it slide. Her breathing had gone shallow at some point, and she was starting to feel light-headed. "This isn't about the shop and our disagreement there, is it?"

"It's about a lot of things, Maddie. But

most importantly, it's about two people who do really well in a false environment."

"You don't think we would do well in a different environment?"

It was the closest she'd come, other than kissing the guy, to indicate that she was thinking of them as a "we." And she was. She had barely admitted it to herself, having instead rocked the myth that they were two people in a temporary situation, just as Sean had said. Was it fair to try to change the rules now?

His gaze was intense as it met hers. "I don't."

Gut punch.

Maddie pressed her lips together. Hard. So hard that they began to feel numb. Sean stepped forward and took her face in his surprisingly warm leather gloves and she allowed her mouth to relax as he leaned in to lightly kiss her lips. The movement was restrained, as if he was afraid of losing control. Then he brought his forehead down to touch hers.

"I'm a guy who does best alone, Maddie. Consider me another bullet dodged."

She pressed her forehead against his, tightened her grip on his sleeves. "I don't want to take the money, Sean." It was easier to address the money than the fact that her heart was breaking.

"But I hope you will," he said softly. "Because I'm asking you to."

She bit her lip then eased back, allowing her hands to fall away. He needed to leave. She read it in his pained expression. Maybe he was leaving due to fear. Or maybe he was truly a lone wolf, meant for a life of solitude.

Did it matter? The result was the same. And she needed to accept that.

CHAPTER FIFTEEN

"THE PLACE SEEMS kind of empty, you know." Dillon pulled out a kitchen chair and sat across from Maddie, who was trying to focus on a holiday-themed crossword puzzle, but was instead staring at black and white squares with a pencil in one hand.

The place did seem empty, even though this was the way things were supposed to be when she'd called Max and asked for a place to stay—her and Dillon manning the ranch in his parents' absence. Sean shouldn't have been in the picture. But he was there when she'd shown up, and he up-ended everything, including her perspective.

"I know," Maddie said. "Big hole."

Before leaving, Sean had spent the morning transferring hay to different areas for easy feeding, double-checking the waterers and even riding the fence on the snowmobile. She knew why he'd been doing those things—lone wolf or not, Sean didn't walk away from commitments—but the fact that he was leaving before Christmas had stunned her. It was only the realization that if she didn't want him butting into her life uninvited, then she had no right to butt into his that kept her from telling him that they could keep out of each other's way until his job really started. After he'd finished, it'd taken him maybe twenty minutes to pack his truck, then he stopped by the lodge for a stilted goodbye to her and Dillon and to mention that he'd lined up James Farley in case there were any emergencies. The arrangement gave her an incentive to make certain no emergencies occurred.

"Well, it isn't like we can't handle the place." Dillon sat at the table, drummed his fingers a few times. He didn't sound happy.

"We are more than capable."

"Sean's really good at fixing things."

And messing things up. For her, anyway.

"He is," Maddie said, the sarcasm in her voice causing Dillon to give her a frowning look.

"What happened?" he asked matter-of-factly. "For real, I mean."

She met the teen's gaze. She knew he was astute, but it was still unnerving when the kid zeroed in on stuff so effortlessly. "In what way?"

"His job doesn't start until January. I know because he told me. Why is he leaving now, instead of staying for Christmas? We'd discussed cooking Christmas tacos and now he's gone."

Maddie gave a casual shrug as she lifted her coffee cup. "He said that he wants to get set up before he starts work. Find a place and all that." She spoke in a manner that sounded legitimately offhand...or so she thought until Dillon replied.

"Right," the kid muttered in a disbelieving note.

Maddie cocked her head. "What do you think is going on?"

Dillon fiddled with fringe on the place mat in front of him and then his fingers stilled. "I think that he's scared. I think the walls are closing in."

Maddie stared at him, having no idea

what he was talking about. Dillon gave her a patient look.

"I think he's happy until he starts thinking about it." Dillon raised his gaze. "You know?"

"I do," Maddie confessed now that she understood what he was getting at. She'd seen the same thing. Whether he had reason to or not, Sean *was* acting like the walls were closing in. When he realized he wasn't on his own, that he liked being in this "fantasyland," as he'd called it, he panicked, probably because fantasylands didn't last forever. And in his panic, he'd thrown up a big wall to keep Maddie at a distance.

Could it be that she was also scaring him?

That gave her pause. If she was, then she wasn't the only one tentatively thinking in terms of "we," and that would help explain Sean's sudden departure. He was getting sucked into a situation he wasn't ready for. Maybe even one he didn't believe he was capable of handling, given his background and failed romances. And he had the handy excuse of Maddie not being ready for a new relationship due to her recent breakup.

"You get what I'm saying?" Dillon finally asked after several seconds of silence.

"Yes," she said slowly. "I think I do."

"Sucks."

"Yes." But it might not be the end of the story. Something was stirring deep inside of Maddie's brain. Small tendrils of hope and possibility were weaving together, not so much in a plan, but into a different perspective.

What would she do with this new perspective?

She lifted her coffee mug. Kat and Whit were coming by on Tuesday for a potluck dinner. It would be a perfect time to explain the situation and get their views on the matter.

Maddie discarded the idea almost as soon as it came into her head. Before tossing things out to her friends, she wanted to be on steadier emotional ground.

And she was afraid of getting answers she didn't want to hear. Logical answers such as, *Are you nuts? Get over one rela-*

tionship before you break your heart with another.

How was it that she was more hurt by losing a relationship that had never been officially acknowledged, than by losing the one she'd spent years building?

She'd keep things to herself. No sense worrying her friends. Maddie set down her cup and studied the lights that twinkled outside the windows as Dillon reached for another cookie and took a bite, chewing with a thoughtful expression on his face.

"This has been a weird Christmas," he said.

"A little." Maddie smiled perfunctorily. Weird. Confusing. Eye-opening.

Maybe Sean was right, and he was another bullet dodged.

But maybe he was wrong…maybe she was ridiculously in love with the man, and needed to do something about it.

"IS THIS YOUR first Christmas away from your parents?" Kat asked Dillon as they sat around the big dining room table, a game of Risk spread out in front of them. Livia,

Troy's baby, slept on a thick blanket on the floor near the tree while the adults indulged in Christmas cheer and world domination.

"Technically, they are away from me," Dillon said before throwing the dice. The kid had some kind of weird luck going on and was about to wipe out Whit's last country. Whit was competitive and didn't want her last country to be wiped out, but it appeared that she was soon to take her place in the cheering section.

He lost the roll, and Whitney perked up.

"But yes. This is the first," he continued, smiling at Kat. "I could fly down for a couple of days, but it doesn't seem worth all the money and hassle of traveling so close to Christmas. Sometimes you've got to make sacrifices."

"I understand," Kat said. "We—" she indicated Whit and Maddie with a wave of her hand "—missed prom every year due to high school rodeo."

"I guess that's why I get such a kick out of selling prom dresses," Maddie said. "I never had one of my own."

She thought she was doing a great job of

acting like she was fine with her new life, relatively happy with the world, on board with the joy of the season.

Too bad her friends weren't buying it.

They hadn't said anything—yet—but she knew them well enough to know they were concerned for her, no doubt because she'd experienced a double—no, make that a triple—whammy. Her broken engagement, her sneaky business partner, Sean financing her escape from said business. If she added in the realization that of all the things that had happened lately, Sean leaving had put the biggest hole in her life, she had a quadruple whammy.

The more she thought about it, the more she was convinced that he'd left because they'd been on the brink of something. It'd been slow growing, but it had been growing. She'd categorized the fragile bond between them as a fun little fling because logic decreed that she needed time to get over her broken engagement. Her heart had disagreed.

It still did. To the point that she'd had a hard time sleeping since Sean had driven away, his few belongings loaded in the back seat of his truck. She'd checked his cabin the day after he left and other than the scent of the soap he'd used, there was nothing left of him there. He'd even emptied the trash. The saddles in the tack shed now gleamed. As far as she knew, he hadn't mothered any orphan kittens, but he had tried to take care of her.

She'd been the one to peg him as a caregiver, later changing it to protector. Both were correct. He'd been her caregiving, protector, who'd bent the rules to help her out, because yes—she would have said no if he'd offered to finance her escape from the business.

"Maddie."

Her gaze jerked up to Whit. "My roll?"

"You're out."

"Right." She leaned back in her chair and Dillon set the dice on the table with a deliberate motion. She glanced around and found that all eyes were on her. "Is this an intervention?"

She meant it as a joke, but it didn't come off as such.

Livia started making fussy noises from where she lay, and Troy pushed back his chair. "I have a diaper to change."

Dillon also pushed back his chair. "I have a cake in the oven."

Maddie raised her eyes skyward, but didn't protest as the two guys left the room, Troy packing his baby, and Dillion dutifully going to the kitchen to see about his pretend cake.

"What's going on?" Kat asked. "What can we do to help?"

Maddie looked past her friends' concerned faces to the tree behind them that she and Sean had decorated, intending to gather her thoughts, but instead being smacked with a memory. They'd kissed next to the tree before the open house started, breaking apart mere seconds before Dillon had bopped into the room, and then she'd kissed him during the open house. She'd spent the evening holding those kisses close, marveling at how they made her feel. It hadn't felt fling-like and perhaps she should have paid more attention.

She missed the man, missed his kisses.

But most of all, she missed the feeling of something special taking root and growing between them. A feeling that refused to pass and felt both different and stronger than what she and Cody had built over the years.

"I'm fine," Maddie said.

"How in the world are you fine?" Whit asked.

"I guess because I have good friends?"

"Is it Sean?" Maddie's heart rate jumped at the accurate guess, then slowed again, when Whit continued, "I know he did a bad thing going behind your back with the business loan, but he was right about you refusing help. You would have, and I think he came up with a decent solution to the problem of what to do about the shop." Whit shot a look at Kat, who interjected.

"Not that you need anyone doing what's best for you without permission."

"I should have had a say," Maddie said, even though the argument sounded tired, probably because she'd repeated it to herself so many times. It was true, but it was also a done deal and instead of rehashing it, she needed to move on.

"Agreed. What are you going to do?" Whit asked, leaning her forearms on the table, mirroring Kat's positions. Maddie did the same, glad that her friends thought this was about the shop.

"I'm not sure."

Whit and Kat exchanged glances, then Kat said, "We thought that maybe we could pool resources and pay Sean back, then he would be released, and you could still be free from the shop and—"

Maddie's expression must had said more than she intended.

"Or not," Whit murmured.

"I appreciate the offer, but…" Her voice trailed as she realized what she needed to do. "I'm going to discuss the matter with Sean."

She was going to lay some things to rest.

"When will you discuss it with Sean?" Whit asked cautiously.

Maddie drew in a breath, then said, "Soon, I guess."

Troy came back from the bedroom where

he'd been hanging out after changing Livia's diaper, giving the friends their privacy. But Livia was still fussing, and it wasn't getting better.

"It's getting late," Kat said. "We should get on home...unless we should stay?"

An offer to continue the conversation if Maddie needed to talk more. She did not.

"I'm good," she said with a smile. "If I don't see you before Christmas, I'll see you soon after."

"Merry Christmas," Dillon chimed in from the kitchen doorway, apparently having sensed that the mood in the house had changed.

"Don't do anything crazy," Kat said as she hugged her goodbye a few minutes later.

"I won't," Maddie promised. It wasn't crazy to have a discussion she hadn't been ready to have before Sean had left. It might be a little crazy to do it in person, but she needed to see him, to read his expression as she addressed the situation that she simply couldn't let lie.

Kat stepped back holding her at arm's length. "How are you going to find him?"

"How do you know I'm not going to simply call him?"

When Kat gave her a "because I know you" look, Maddie felt her cheeks go warm. Busted.

"I'm going to ask him where he is."

Kat and Whit exchanged looks. "That's kind of brilliant," Whit said.

"Let me know if you need help with chores." Kat inclined her head toward Whit. "We'll both help, you know."

"I know," Maddie said softly. "And thanks, but James is on call."

Kat's lips twitched, but she didn't say anything about her brother. Instead she said, "If you need additional help, give a yell."

"You know," Troy added from where he was putting Livia in her snowsuit. "Like help putting out a fire or something."

After the two sets of taillights had disappeared down the driveway, Maddie turned from the window to find Dillon regarding her from the kitchen doorway, where he leaned against the frame in a casual pose.

"What's the plan?" he asked.

Maddie didn't even blink at the question. "I'm going to find Sean and bring him home for Christmas—if he'll come, that is."

"You might have to get tough," Dillon replied, obviously approving. "I'd offer to come along as backup, but—"

"Someone has to keep an eye on James Farley."

Dillon gave her a look. "I was going to say that I didn't want to be a third wheel."

Maddie smiled. "Maybe that, too."

She hoped.

SEAN FINALLY PUT a name to the feeling that had dogged him since he'd driven away from the Lucky Creek Ranch.

He was lonely.

He missed his pretend family, which was nuts because—hey—it was a pretend family. A temporary thing. What he'd been afraid of, and tried to avoid, had caught up with him. He and Dillon and Maddie had been three people working together for a cause. It hadn't helped that they'd been doing it during what many considered a magical time of year; a time when people pretended all kinds of things and indulged in behaviors that couldn't hold up over the course of the year. That was why holidays were special. They were not sustainable, nor was Sean's ability to be part of a family. If he needed any verification of that, all he had to do was to look around. There he was in a darkish motel room, not a tree or bauble or candy cane in sight. He'd chosen this, his reality, rather than allowing his hopes to run high concerning his ability to carve out a new kind of life.

And now he had to deal with Maddie, who'd given him little choice but to deal with her. She'd told him via text message just how things would be—like it or not, he was going to see her.

Of course he wanted to see her, even if it tore his heart out. The hard part was going to be convincing her of what the future needed to look like.

Sean paced the length of his motel room, then back again, part of him wishing he'd been less honest, another part saying that this was something that needed to happen. Apparently, they both needed more closure than the goodbye kiss by the tractor had given them. When she'd texted him, asking where he was, in the name of honesty he'd told her. He hadn't expected her next text to be I'm coming to see you.

She must have then turned off her phone because she didn't reply to his text telling her not to. And since he'd loaned money to her business partner behind her back, he decided that the least he could do was to see her if she drove from Larkspur to Visage, Montana, on the Wyoming border, where he'd holed up while waiting for his job to officially start in ten days. He'd gotten a good rate at the motel because the holidays were slow in the little town, and he didn't mind Christmas alone. He could use the hot plate in his room to make dinner on the day, when everything would be closed, and until then, the café offered decent meals.

Decent, lonely meals.

Never in his life had he felt so adrift, or on edge, which was ridiculous because he wasn't adrift. He had a job pending, plans to attend school in a year. He had goals.

And a hole in his life.

The phone rang and as soon as he said hello, his heart hammering more than it should have been, the motel manager said, "I have a lady here asking about you."

"I'll be right there."

He stepped out of the room into a crisp white world capped by a pale blue sky. The motel parking lot was edged with high snowbanks pushed up by the plow, and the wind blew snow and a few pieces of paper across the lot. Classic Wyoming winter, even though he was still in Montana.

He spotted Maddie's truck parked on the far side of the office and sucked in a breath. For better or worse, they were doing this.

He started toward the truck only to stop when the office door opened and Maddie stepped out, only yards away from him.

Yards that felt like miles...until they didn't.

Sean didn't know what he'd expected— other than the worst—but it hadn't been for the feeling of distance and separation and mile-high barriers to melt like the snow in a puddle. He needed to rebuild those barriers, STAT—for her sake as much as for his. They had to be realistic. Just because he wanted something, it didn't mean he should have it…or that he wouldn't screw it up if he got it.

His legs didn't get the message. They kept moving toward her, causing him to believe that he needed to put some heavy work into rebuilding his self-control. There'd been a time when he'd understood his limitations and hadn't let himself get drawn into thinking he was someone he wasn't, or capable of things he was not. But Maddie hadn't been heading toward him during those times, a determined expression on her face that made him feel a little bit afraid.

She came to a stop a few feet away, close enough that he was able to get a whiff of floral perfume on the cool breeze, but far enough away that he couldn't touch her.

He ached to touch her, which was why he kept his hands at his sides, his fingers balled in loose fists.

"I figured it out."

Sean blinked at her. "What?"

She pushed her hands into her pockets, shifting her weight as she did so. "I think you discovered that you liked *not* being alone and it scared the crap out of you."

Obviously there would be no beating around the bush or polite conversation, or even getting in out of the cold. They were doing this thing here and now.

"I…uh…"

What was he supposed to say when confronted with the truth—a truth he'd truly believed only he was privy to?

Now he shifted his weight. "What of it?"

Lame, lame, lame.

She gave him a long look, and it was only because he now knew her so well, better than he'd intended, that he recognized that she was nervous. And that took a bit of the edge off his own nerves.

"I never took you for a coward."

His chin snapped up. "I'm not a coward."

"I think you have feelings for me, and that caused you to run."

Oh crap.

"You were engaged to be married less than a month ago."

"And we both know what a mistake that was." She raised her eyebrows. "Cody and I did everything right. We dated for two years before we got engaged, took the time to be certain we weren't making a mistake…but we were."

"What's your point, Maddie?" The words came out on a cool note, but inside he was dying.

"My point." She pursed her lips and glanced down, causing a wave of insecurity to blast through him before logic smacked him a couple of times and told him she wouldn't have driven this many miles to say that she didn't care about him. She met his gaze. "My point is that sometimes we think we're doing the right thing. It's all very logical and sane and respectful of time-tested traditions…but it's wrong because *we* were wrong about what we needed." She lifted her chin. "Now I'm sure of what I need."

"Maddie…" The gruffly pleading tone of his voice didn't stop her.

"I love you, Sean Arteaga."

He'd suspected, but now that she'd said the

words aloud, he felt like he'd been smacked by a truck. It felt good.

"Come here," he said roughly. "Come here and say that again."

He didn't need to ask twice. She came to him, nearly taking him down as she launched herself into his arms. But she didn't take him down. And she wouldn't. Not unless she left him again. He laughed and swung her around, awkwardly because of his bum leg, then buried his face in her soft hair.

"I love you so much," he murmured. She pressed herself more tightly against him, holding him the way he needed to be held. The way he was going to allow himself to be held from this moment on.

For the longest time they stood, his face pressed against her sweet-smelling hair. Then he found her lips, or maybe she found his.

It was only when a chill blast of wind hit them that he recalled they were standing in the cold on the Montana-Wyoming border, in December, no less. He eased himself away from her, hanging on to her shoulders so as not to lose contact. He needed contact in a way that would have frightened him if it hadn't been Maddie that he needed to touch. The woman he loved and trusted.

"I want you to come home," she said. "Christmas won't be the same without you."

"Do we have to do a bunch of analysis and stuff?"

"No. I think the 'I love you, you love me' is analysis enough."

He could get on board with that. His arms tightened around her again. "Life isn't the same without you." He pulled her close. "What about the shop and trust and all that? I overstepped."

"But you would do it again."

"Maybe. But only because—"

She kissed him in a way that told him the discussion was shelved.

She pulled in a shaky breath as she stepped back. "Get your stuff. We're going home."

"Maddie." He ran his hands over the upper part of her jacket sleeves. "I have to work this job."

"I know," she said simply. "But not until your start date."

He let out a breath. Did he want to spend his holidays in a motel room when he could be with his pretend family, which it seemed, was more real than he'd ever imagined? Family, it appeared, was a state of mind.

"It won't take me long," he said.

As they walked to their separate vehicles after he'd tossed his stuff into his duffel and checked out of the room, he realized that this was his first real second chance. He hadn't had one with his previous relationships—hadn't even known a second chance was a possibility…but he had one now.

And that was huge.

"I hate driving separately," Maddie said as they stopped at his truck.

He smiled down at her. "You lead and I'll follow. We'll get there together regardless of how we travel."

She reached up to cup the scarred side of his face with her gloved palm. "That we will."

CHAPTER SIXTEEN

"THIS IS MY best ever Christmas Eve," Sean said with a lazy smile as Maddie handed him a mug of cider laced with bourbon. Dillon was arranging cookies on a plate after finishing a video call with his parents and Sean took advantage of the kid's absence to pull a small package out from behind the cushion of the sofa and hand it to her.

Maddie gave him a stricken look. "I got you nothing, as per orders." Except for the small train set that was on back order. She planned to surprise him in January when she visited him in Wyoming. Not that a night calver had a lot of time or room to set up a train, but she figured it was the thought that mattered. And they could set it up later—maybe next Christmas.

"You got me everything," he said gruffly.

"You're getting poetic in your old age," Maddie said.

"No need to be insulting," he murmured, sliding an arm around her. Maddie was never going to get tired of snuggling with this guy, but she sat up a little straighter as she turned the package over in her hands. "I'll open it tomorrow."

"It's a token. You can open it now."

She pulled the ribbon and lifted the lid. Inside was a blown glass ornament. A sun with pointy rays. "It's beautiful." She gave him a look. "Maddie Sunshine?"

He shrugged. "My poetic self couldn't resist."

Her lips parted and she started to lean close when Dillon said from the kitchen doorway, "Here now. None of that. At least not in front of impressionable minds."

"So what do you think of Maddie's idea," Dillon asked after placing the plate of cookies on the table, and then taking a seat in the chair opposite the sofa with a mug of what had better be virgin cider in his hands. The teen must have read Maddie's mind because he said, "Lips that touch liquor will never touch mine."

She felt Sean laugh, but his voice was matter-of-fact when he said, "I'm going along with Maddie's plan. I think it's a great idea."

"Sean Arteaga. World Champion Bronc Rider. Locally Renowned Bridal Shop Owner." Dillon pretended to consider. "It has a ring to it."

That it did. And after having a sit-down with Kayla on Christmas Eve, the day after Maddie had followed her gut and brought Sean back where he belonged for Christmas, they'd decided that Sean would buy Kayla out.

Maddie had been stunned that her former partner had been amenable to the idea, but come to find out, she'd been thinking of leaving Larkspur. Maddie had no idea if Cody was going with her, and she didn't care. She had her shop back, and since Sean would be a silent partner, she would handle things the way she'd always wanted to. Sean was going to take his diesel course the following year, and they would see where life took them.

Was it a mistake going into business with a guy she'd fallen for?

Logically it might be, but her heart was clear on the matter. She was making the right decision. She met Sean's gaze, and he in turn gave Dillon a "don't say a word" look before meeting her lips with a short, sweet, promise-filled kiss.

"I can't believe I'm giving this up to pull calves in below-zero weather," he murmured against her lips.

"And you'll be back here for spring calving," she said.

"Thanks to me," Dillon said smugly.

"Thank you, Dillon," Sean replied. The teen had put in a word with his dad, who had in turn convinced Sean that they needed him on the guest ranch until his class started next January. He would deal solely with livestock, not guests, which had made the decision to stay a no-brainer. Besides, if people went out of their way to help, he was going to accept graciously—just as Maddie had finally accepted his help with the bridal shop by making him a partner.

"The weather here will seem balmy by comparison," Maddie pointed out. "Not counting the April blizzards, of course."

"I can't wait. Balmy weather, a nice cabin—"

"Lair, Sean. We call them lairs."

Their gazes held until Dillon cleared his throat. "Mistletoe is over there." He pointed to the doorway.

Maddie laughed and scooted away from Sean. "We're good."

"For now," Sean murmured, low enough so only she could hear. "Where's that Risk game?"

"About time." Dillon got to his feet and picked up the plate of cookies, heading to the game table set up at the far side of the room.

Sean took advantage of the moment of semiprivacy to say, "Thank you for bringing me home, Maddie."

She put her hand on his cheek. "Thank you for coming back to us."

His expression softened, but his gaze was intense as he said, "We can do it, you know."

"What?"

He slid a hand around the back of her neck, pulling her lips closer to his own. "We can make a happy ending."

"Who are you?" she asked in mock amazement just before he kissed her in a way that made it impossible to do anything but what she'd done for most of her life.

She believed.

* * * * *